About the author

Dr. Gerloch retired in 1999 from a career as an academic and research scientist in the field of quantum chemistry in the University of Cambridge. He is an emeritus fellow of Trinity Hall. He and his wife, Gwyneth, have since lived in Canberra, Australia. During his first twenty years of blissful retired domesticity, Malcolm has enjoyed gardening, house renovation and above all, learning to cook in several cuisines. Gwyneth has relinquished the kitchen with mixed feelings. Prior to writing children's books, Malcolm's greatest achievement has been the construction of a dual-manual harpsichord for his wife to play. That was a present to thank her for introducing him to the non-scientific literature of – mostly – the nineteenth and twentieth century European and twentieth century North American writers.

OLD HARALD
AND OTHER STORIES

Malcolm Gerloch

**OLD HARALD
AND OTHER STORIES**

Vanguard Press

VANGUARD PAPERBACK

© Copyright 2020
Malcolm Gerloch

The right of Malcolm Gerloch to be identified as author of
this work has been asserted by him in accordance with the
Copyright, Designs and Patents Act 1988.

All Rights Reserved

No reproduction, copy or transmission of this publication
may be made without written permission.
No paragraph of this publication may be reproduced,
copied or transmitted save with the written permission of the publisher, or in
accordance with the provisions
of the Copyright Act 1956 (as amended).

Any person who commits any unauthorised act in relation to
this publication may be liable to criminal
prosecution and civil claims for damages.

A CIP catalogue record for this title is
available from the British Library.

ISBN 978 1 784658 97 7

*Vanguard Press is an imprint of
Pegasus Elliot MacKenzie Publishers Ltd.*
www.pegasuspublishers.com

First Published in 2020

**Vanguard Press
Sheraton House Castle Park
Cambridge England**

Printed & Bound in Great Britain

Dedication

I hope that I have inherited just one small part of the steel with which my mother grappled with life. I think of her often with love, admiration and gratitude and I dedicate these stories to her memory.

Acknowledgements

I thank my wife, Gwyneth, for her love and endless patience in reading and rereading the manuscript and for her advice and suggestions.

CONTENTS

OLD HARALD 13
The Meet 15
Reunion 22
The Verdict 28
    VOICES 31
Details 34
Cross Currents 42
Impulse to Join 46
    EXPECTATIONS 49
The Tramp 51
Pow Wow 57
A Present 61
A Wider Audience 62
    RANT 65
My Musical Groin 67
Some Balance 70
Must I Choose? 74
    BROTHER, SISTER, HUSBAND, WIFE 77
PART 1 HONOR and ARNO 79
    Putting on the Dog 81
    Across the Pennines 92
    Out of the Blue 97
    A Plan 101
    Knew it All Along 103
PART 2 BILL and LEAH 107
    Getting Settled 109
    The Poor Relations 121

A Sense of Shame 124
    EXTRA CURRICULAR 131
Early On 133
High Fidelity 139
Two French Masters 144
Some of Life's Little Coincidences 147
A Mate on the Right 151
Keep an Eye Open... 153
Who Guards the Guards? 156
Art Club... 159
Posh Digs 162
Growing Up... 165
Sophistication... 168
Sad News and Old Friends.............................. 171
    DOWN TO EARTH...175
    A LIKELY STORY 187
Playing the Numbers 189
A Caring Man.. 192
Make Like an Egyptian 195
Soul Mates... 199
Confessions 203
The Cosmic Lottery... 206
Unlikely Junk 211

OLD HARALD

The Meet

It happens. There are days when Harry gets lonely and miserable. He is a bachelor and lives on his own. If he feels out of sorts, he can deal with it in his own way. He needs nobody's permission. He can just hear his friends and family chastising him for his choices but so what.

He went off one afternoon to his favourite watering hole in town and sat down at the bar. It's amazing how many wonderful things can happen in a bar. And some are true.

'Same old, same old, Joe,' he greeted the barman and wondered if that really was his name. Joe had told him it was but can you really believe all you hear in a bar? The ever-efficient Joe promptly delivered his usual cocktail, complete with an olive stuck on the end of a cocktail stick, which formed the support of a miniature paper umbrella – a swizzle stick, for God's sake.

Harry didn't like talking much when he was in one of these moods. Joe was a wise and experienced barman; he understood and left him alone. Don't get the wrong idea. Harry might get a bit morose occasionally, but he's no drunk. He sipped very slowly so that his martini would last for ages. No, he just liked the place, the old-fashioned décor, the lighting, the jazz playing softly in the background. No roughs came into this bar. Swizzle sticks were a small price to pay for a little tranquillity. He could be sure of a quiet time whilst he bemoaned his fate. Not that he really had anything to complain about. He just thought he was entitled to be pissed off all on his own now and again. It's a free country, he mused. And anyway, he didn't do this very often.

Usually, he would mope alone. Nobody joined him, probably because the set of his back clearly said, "Leave me alone!" Anyway, that's *usually*. Today turned out to be different. He paid little attention when a shadow appeared on his right as somebody sat down on the stool next to his.

Oh, don't do that, thought Harry, There are plenty of empty stools along the bar. Why bother me? Sometimes it's good to be bothered, Harry.

'I hope you don't mind my joining you,' said a soft but respectful female voice, 'but I really could do with a little conversation, if you wouldn't mind too much.' Not too pushy but a touch pleading.

He looked at the speaker for a moment. She was a nice-enough looking lady – actually rather better than that, he thought as he focussed more clearly – well-dressed, middle-aged like himself and wearing a sufficiently neutral expression on her face to dispel any concern for his privacy.

'Not at all,' Harry politely lied, 'but I'm afraid I'm not good company right now.'

'Nor me,' she replied, 'so we can be miserable so-and-sos together!'

She didn't over-push herself or the conversation. Joe brought her a cocktail not unlike Harry's – well it had an olive on the end of a little paper umbrella, at least – even though Harry hadn't heard her give her order. They sat in silence for a while before each, separately and independently, suddenly felt embarrassed and just had to break the silence. As is so often the way, they began speaking together.

'I'm sorry,' Harry said, 'I don't think I've seen you in here before.'

As he said it, he realised how like "Do you come here often?" that sounded and he laughed sheepishly. But by then, she had blurted out:

'I don't often do this, you know,' and immediately thought how like a teenager she sounded.

'Shall we start again?' Harry offered. 'I'm Harry. I tend to come in here when I'm a bit out of sorts.'

'I can't claim to have done this before,' she replied. 'My name's Marian. Hello, Harry! I have my own reasons for feeling put out today and it's so nice to hear a voice that isn't shouting in my brain.'

'I promise not to shout,' Harry assured her, and she could believe it for his voice sounded as if he always spoke quietly, not in an unsure whisper but calmly and clearly. Not a boring voice, mind you, for he could become quite animated when something excited him but his nature just didn't allow him to shout.

Neither of them asked the other what bothered them that day. It was clearly understood that each considered that an intrusion into the other's privacy.

'I rather like the music here,' Marian said after a while. 'I guess that this sort of stuff isn't too popular these days. It reminds me a bit of the old bebop era. I wasn't around then, obviously, but I always gravitated to that older style of jazz when I was a kid.' That confirmed Harry's estimate of her age!

'Me too,' Harry replied. 'A schoolmate of mine introduced me to this cool stuff. I remember how I thought it too clever and difficult at first but I grew to love it as he lent me more and more of his precious records. Hey! There's a word you don't hear much anymore – at least not to do with music. Everyone downloads these days!'

'Did you like the Modern Jazz Quartetand Gerry Mulligan?' Marian asked.

'Oh yeah!' he said. 'And Duke Ellington. And Ella Fitzgerald! Thelonious Monk, Miles Davis.'

Harry was beginning to enjoy himself. He hadn't thought about those musicians for years. The music they were listening to now, playing softly through the various loudspeakers around the bar was hardly in the same league but at least it provided a nostalgic atmosphere. They were silent for a while, sharing.

'I hope you don't mind my asking,' said Marian after a while, 'but what line of work are you in?'

'I write children's books,' Harry said.

'Goodness,' she replied, 'I'd never have guessed that.'

'Why not?' asked Harry. 'Couldn't you see my tail or hear me purr?'

'No no, I know it's silly to imagine that there are stereotypes for every occupation. It's just that I've met people from many walks of life before – including an author once – but never a writer of children's books. Is it very hard?'

Harry smiled a little wistfully. 'Sometimes it is. I have been stuck on a topic for weeks – even longer – but then sometimes, it just flows out almost without stopping. I can never tell how it's going to be when I begin a new book.'

'What's your surname, Harry?'

'Very boring and apt, I'm afraid; it's Old,' he replied, with a grin. 'Harry Old. You won't have heard of that name, though, because I publish under a scrambled pseudonym in praise of my hero.'

She looked at him, quizzically.

'Old Harald,' he said and waited.

There was quite a long pause before she said, 'I do believe that I've seen some of your books. Indeed, I think I once gave one to a niece. I have no children of my own.' She hastened on. 'I'm not married.'

'Not necessary these days,' Harry came back.

'No,' she said, 'but it's true anyway. The reason I was quiet for so long just now is—'

'That you were going to ask me if I did crosswords,' he interrupted.

'Yes, exactly.'

Harry was beginning to enjoy this lady's quick-thinking conversation. 'It's a good question, of course, but actually I don't!'

'Oh well,' she said, 'I don't suppose it's mandatory.'

'No, but you got it right though,' said Harry with a grin. 'Not many people are as quick as that.'

Now it was Marian's turn to be pleased with the way the chat was progressing and flashed a little smile in acknowledgement. 'Do you find it very difficult to simplify things sufficiently for kids to understand you?'

'I do and I don't,' he replied. 'Or, rather, I do try to do that sometimes but then sometimes I don't. I think that children are far cleverer and more understanding than many adults believe. If kids lack anything, it's likely to be a degree of subtlety in their understanding of complex emotions. How could it be otherwise when most have not lived long enough to have experienced many emotions, those to do with growing up and puberty, for a start. But they can usually tell right from wrong, they know about hope and loss, and for sure, they know far more about most technical matters than do adults. Just think about setting up your mobile phone, for example!'

'Tell me,' Marian came back. 'What's the most difficult thing you've tried to explain to a child?'

Harry mused for a moment.

'Well, I'll tell you about something I cut out of a story once because of pressure from some friends who thought I'd gone way over the top.'

'Try me,' Marian replied.

'OK. I won't go through the main story because that would take too long and it isn't necessary to make my point anyway,' began Harry.

'Imagine a mother and her daughter, Anna – eight years old, say. They are out in their garden, looking at some interesting birds on the branch of a tree some way off. Anna asks her mum,

"Do birds think like we do, Mummy? Do they feel happy and sad?"

"Well," Mum replies. "You must be careful not to get too anthropomorphic about this."

"What's annamorfik?" the daughter replies, struggling girl-fully with the pronunciation of this strange word.

"No, Anna, the word is *anthropo-morphic*. The *morphic* part comes from an ancient Greek word meaning *in the shape of* and—"

"What's ancient Greek?" interrupts Anna.

"It's a language from long ago which isn't spoken these days but much of our language is based upon it," her mother valiantly tries to explain. "Anyway, the *anthropo* part comes from another ancient Greek word meaning, *human*. So when you put the two halves together, you get *anthropomorphic* to mean *in the form of humans*. We use the word here to mean that we shouldn't look at birds – or animals or fishes, for that matter – in the same way that we look at people." '

Harry paused.

'Hmm,' Marian said somewhat dubiously. 'I'm not too sure that even ten-year-olds would get that.'

'Ah, but wait! There's more still,' Harry continued, warming to his task. 'Up on the tree branch, one bird is asking the other,

"Do humans think like we do? Do they feel happy and sad?" '

'Oh, I like that reversal,' Marian interjected.

Harry continued. '"Well," says the older, more experienced bird, "You must be careful not to get too *poulimorphic* about this."

"What's *pollymorfik*?" asked the younger bird, trying its best.

"No, the word is *pouli-morphic*. The *morphic* parts comes from an ancient Greek word meaning *in the shape of* and—"

"What's ancient Greek?" interrupts the youngster.

"It's a language from long ago which isn't spoken these days but much of our language is based upon it," the older bird says, patiently, and continues. "The *pouli* part comes from another ancient Greek word, *poulos*, meaning, *bird*. So when you put the two halves together, you get *poulimorphic* to mean *in the form of birds*. We use the word here to mean that we shouldn't look at humans – or animals or fishes – in the same way that we look at birds." '

Marian put her hand on Harry's arm. 'This is getting very involved.' She giggled.

'Ah! You are not the only one to feel that way,' Harry conceded. 'I put all this to a friend of a friend some time ago, a mother of a ten-year-old, more or less I think, and she not only complained about the difficulty of her child getting her head around anthropomorphic but went on to say that while she had checked that the word did indeed exist, by looking it up in the dictionary, she'd also tried unsuccessfully to find the word *poulimorphic* in the dictionary; indeed, she went further, claiming to have consulted several of the world's major dictionaries. I had to reply to my friend, the intermediary, well, it's in the Bird Dictionary! She should have looked there!'

Marian was in fits. 'Oh, I do like that; but I still think it was all too difficult.'

Harry grinned ruefully. 'Well, maybe I agree with you because I cut it all out in the final version. But I was sorry because I so enjoyed myself while I was writing it and I do believe that my sense of humour now isn't so very different from what it was when I was ten.' He added, 'I have been having so much fun.'

Harry offered Marian another drink and signalled to the barman. Two more paper umbrella swizzle sticks arrived.

'Do you always write about birds, Harry?' asked Marian.

'Oh no! I have written about cats and dogs, an echidna, spiders and dragonflies – all sorts of things. I once wrote a sort of crime story in which a houseful of teddy bears argued the toss, all speaking at the same time. I remember telling an old friend of mine about all this and sending him copies for his input. He liked my stories about birds and cats but drew the line at stuffed animals talking. This guy is a great friend of mine and a university professor, for heaven's sake. He objected to conversations between soft toys but was perfectly willing to swallow tales of birds and cats chewing the fat! It's funny where people want to draw the line. I told him – out of bravado, I suppose – that I could make anything speak.'

'Really, Harry?' Marian challenged. 'Do you really think you can?'

'I *think* I can,' Harry replied, 'and I'm not the only one who has thought so. Think of the film *Toy Story*, for example, or *Paddington*. I hadn't seen that when I wrote my tale about the teddy bears but the idea is much the same. I doubt whether there's a new idea under the sun. Many musicians, for example, pinch ideas, not only from others' work but from their own as well. Balzac had a lot to say about the usefulness of plagiarism in literature nearly two hundred years ago. There are so many examples. Tell you what,' he said, really warming to his subject now, 'let's meet up here next week and I'll present you with a piece in which these ridiculous swizzle sticks holding on to the olives in our martinis become alive and, maybe even talk!'

'That's really going a bit far, Harry.' Marian laughed. 'But I would like to see that.'

'It's a deal,' Harry said. 'It has been a real pleasure meeting you. You have cheered me up enormously.'

'And you, me,' she replied.

Harry got up. 'I'm sorry, but I have to go now. See you here in seven days!' He held Marian's hand for a moment or so; then he was gone.

I didn't have to leave right then, he thought, but once I get an idea, I simply must get home and think about it. Anyway, it was probably a good idea to quit before I made a fool of myself.

What an afternoon it had turned out to be. He dimly realised that he rather liked this lady.

Reunion

Harry was feeling unusually excited as he walked into the bar one week later. Would Marian actually come? Goodness, he was behaving as if he were a kid. He hadn't felt like this for some time. It was galling in a way but energising at the same time. He sat down at the counter and nodded to Joe who brought him a martini – complete with the obligatory miniature umbrella and olive. Instead of adopting his usual slumped position and air of depression, however, Harry sat upright and looked around the room, and towards the door, in anticipation of seeing his new friend. On the other hand, he was preparing himself mentally for disappointment – just in case.

He had to wait twenty minutes before Marian appeared. She was a little out of breath as she apologised for being late. 'Sorry, Harry, I had an unexpected phone call from someone in trouble. I just had to attend to it.'

'Don't worry,' Harry replied, 'I'm just so pleased you could make it at all.'

He kissed her cheek. She smiled warmly at him. He ordered her a drink and she came to the point immediately. 'Well, have you done it? Am I going to hear from a swizzle stick?'

Harry grinned at her. 'Oh, yes, I rather think you are, although I must admit that I had to think a long while before I could do my thing. I have my little story here and, if you don't mind, I'll read it aloud to you, but before I do, I must confess to being influenced by the title – but only the title – of a delightful piece of music written by Elena Kats-Chernin. It's called *Dance of the Paper Umbrellas*. I must confess that I had heard neither the music nor the title before the other day but was immediately struck by both. I have copied her piece onto a USB stick and have asked our barman here to play it for us while I read. Her title, of course, refers to umbrellas, but seeing those ridiculous swizzle sticks in our glasses last week reminded me of their much larger cousins which was why I suggested doing this in the first place!'

Marian took a sip of her drink. So did Harry. They clinked their glasses together. The swizzle sticks caught up on each other and rotated.

'Go ahead,' Marian said. Joe changed his music as Harry signalled and took out a few pieces of paper from his pocket. He began to read.

"Jerry was feeling out of sorts and decided to visit his favourite bar again. He sat down at the counter and, without a word being spoken, Joe the bartender poured him a martini. As usual, Joe added an olive stuck on the end of a rather sissy sort of swizzle stick. Not only was the stick in the form of a miniature umbrella but it was coloured pale blue. Jerry had complained before about how ill-chosen this colour was; obviously, as far as he was concerned, if you had to put up with such things, at least a pale yellow or olive-green colour would have been more appropriate, *artistic-wise*.

Joe had informed him that the choice was blue or pink. 'Blue for a boy, pink for a girl.'

'You're kidding,' Jerry had said but accepted the blue one with somewhat bad grace. He hardly noticed the swizzle sticks any more. You get used to things. He had barely taken a sip when he was joined by a rather striking woman, probably of about his own age, he thought. Jerry was somewhat surly at first, simply because he only came to sit in this place to escape the world for an hour or two while he had a sulk about something or other. And he preferred his own company. His companion, however, apologised for disturbing his peace, craving his indulgence because she too was feeling a little blue, and unlike Jerry, preferred someone else's company to her own when she was down. She too ordered a martini and it too came with the inevitable swizzle stick in an olive. But hers, of course, was pink. Joe knew his job.

She sipped; he sipped; they talked.

They chatted about the weather and other trivia until they fell silent out of boredom with themselves. After quite a while, they both started speaking at once, apologising for the banality of their first try at conversation. This time, it went much better and she introduced herself as Marsha. She asked Jerry what he did for a living and he told her he was a professional magician. In reply to Jerry's enquiry, she confessed to being a percussionist in the local orchestra. They were intrigued with each other's professions and began regaling each other with odd and funny stories about people and things they had encountered in their jobs. After some while, Jerry began to realise that his interest in Marsha was blossoming. She had a lovely face and a wicked grin and she seemed rather clever. Jerry thought he saw a somewhat similar interest from her. He certainly hoped so. They were laughing a lot together and Jerry's depression was forgotten completely.

'What pieces is your orchestra playing at the moment?' asked Jerry.

'Well, lots, really but we open, for example, with a short piece by Elena Kats-Chernin called *Dance of the Paper Umbrellas*. I have quite a bit to do in that, of course, because Kats-Chernin is fond of percussion – marimbas, xylophones and so on, particularly coupled with the harp; and, of course, she is a first-rate pianist herself as well as a composer. I love her stuff.'

'Me too,' replied Jerry. 'Let's drink to Elena!'

They clinked their glasses and, as they did, their swizzle sticks got caught up and revolved, one against the other. A slight effervescence from their olives seemed to accompany this fond entanglement while the cocktail sticks loosened themselves from the olives. The freed umbrellas rose a little in their glasses, twirled and seemed to dance around one another, the pink parasol dipping to one side as the blue one became more erect.

'Did you just see that?' asked Marsha. 'Those swizzle sticks seemed to be aware of one another.'

'I think it's in the air right now,' Jerry replied, looking very closely at her.

They put down their glasses on the bar but couldn't help glancing back at them from time to time. The glasses were still now. So were the drinks inside. But the parasols gently rolled around the rims of their glasses. At first, they came together in an effort, it seemed, to touch, but the glasses were too far apart. Marsha thought she heard a gentle sigh as small bubbles appeared from the bottom of her glass. The pink umbrella rose a little in its glass, twirled and began to roll clockwise around the glass. After a couple of rotations, the blue umbrella began to roll around its glass but in an anticlockwise orbit. This went on in a lazy fashion for several rounds until, without any external interference, both swizzle sticks came to rest at the nearest point to one another and pointing their tops one to the other.

'Did you feel a draft?' Jerry asked Marsha.

'Oh, come on,' she said in disbelief. 'This is one of your magic tricks, isn't it?'

Jerry shook his head. 'I wish it were,' he replied.

'Well, whatever caused that, it was rather beautiful,' Marsha said.

'They're a bit like us, don't you think?' replied Jerry, and Marsha touched his hand. They were each about to take another sip of their martinis – their hands had almost reached the glasses – when both drinks fizzed a little, and the umbrellas rose in their confines, rotated and began to move in unison. Both dipped to the left and rotated clockwise; then stopped and rotated the other way while dipping to the right.

'It's like a *pas de deux*!' Marsha gasped, gripping Jerry's hand in her excitement. 'Just what will they do next?'

'I think they like each other,' Jerry said.

In the cocktail glasses, the two swizzle sticks were deep in conversation. The pink parasol was asking the blue, 'Do you think these people are like us? They do seem to like each other.'

The blue umbrella sagely replied, 'You must never assume too much. It is folly to be too *omprelamorphic.*'

'What's *omprelamorphic*?' asked the pink one.

'Well, *morphic* comes from the ancient Greek language and means, *in the shape or form of* while—'

'What's ancient Greek?' interrupted the other.

'It's a language from long ago which isn't spoken these days but much of our language is based upon it,' replied the blue umbrella with some impatience. 'And, anyway, *omprela* is rooted in Greek and means, surprise, surprise... umbrella! So *omprela-morphic* means something like *like umbrellas*!' "

Harry grinned while interrupting his story to say, 'I bet you didn't know the Greeks had a word for umbrella, Marian!'

She was beside herself, in stitches, enjoying every twist and turn of this outrageous yarn. She couldn't speak. 'To be fair, it's only from contemporary Greek!' he admitted. Harry went back to his little tale.

"Jerry and Marsha had finished their drinks quite a while ago but they hadn't noticed, so enthralled with the swizzle display were they. Joe quietly brought two more cocktails and was about to remove the empty glasses when a gentle breeze hit the counter, coming from seemingly nowhere and both of the used swizzle sticks were caught up in it and rose a few centimetres, rotated gently and joined the new parasols in the fresh glasses.

'It's getting a bit crowded in there!' remarked Jerry and ate his olive so freeing the new umbrella. Marsha wiped tears from her eyes with a tissue – tears of unrestrained laughter and joy – and popped her own olive into her mouth.

'There!' she said. 'Everybody's free now.'

On cue, the two pink parasols began rolling around Marsha's glass, following one another clockwise and spinning anticlockwise as they did so. Almost simultaneously, the blue umbrellas followed suit but rotating and spinning in the opposite sense. Marsha thought she could hear a soft gurgling sound coming from the glasses.

'They seem so happy and joyous,' she said to Jerry, becoming quiet and awestruck. Her tears were of a different kind now as she became consumed by the wonder of the dance before them. 'Oh, Jerry, it's so beautiful!' she whispered. Jerry put his arm around her shoulders and she leaned in towards him. They were both mesmerised by the display put on for them.

'I think we've got them hooked now,' one of the swizzle sticks was saying. 'It's amazing how little it takes to get these humans going. Come on, you guys, it's time for the grand finale. Let's really show 'em!'

All four parasols began to spin, gently at first, but with increasing speed. So fast did they spin that, like a squadron of helicopters, they rose into the air, freeing themselves from the constraints of the cocktail glasses. They formed up into a circle above the glasses, having redistributed themselves into a pattern of alternate blue and pink, and spinning all the while, processed as a group in the circle they had formed. Then, while all this was going on, by speeding up or slowing down their individual spins, they oscillated up and down in pairs. As the two pink swizzles rose, the two blue ones fell a little – followed by the reverse.

'This is great!' one of the parasols was saying with great glee.

'We've never done this *pas de quatre* so well before. Just a few moments more now, you guys!'

The excitement in the air was palpable to every creature – to the swizzle sticks who were laughing and to Jerry and Marsha who were sitting in absolute silence as the wonder reached its climax.

'Now!' the umbrellas seemed to say. There was a brief but enormous increase in the rate of spin and all four parasols leaped upwards together, stopped spinning and fell in a heap on the bar. But, even the heap was quite obviously choreographed, for the umbrellas came to rest as pairs, blue with pink, with their sticks crossed. Marsha and Jerry couldn't help themselves. They just exploded with joy, clapping their hands as hard as they could go. Joe, who had been washing and polishing glasses at the other end of the long bar, looked up sharply in some amazement. He'd seen couples getting on together many times before but this was a new one on him.

'Nuts!' he grunted and went back to his polishing.

'Oh, Jerry!' Marsha was saying. 'That was wonderful. I cannot remember seeing a display like it. Was it real? Did we both see it? Did we just imagine it?'

'Well I certainly saw it too,' said Jerry. 'Maybe it's something in the cocktails!'

The Verdict

Harry folded the sheets of paper from which he'd been reading and replaced them in his pocket. He took a sip of his cocktail before saying, 'I could have gone on longer, I suppose, but enough is enough, eh?'

Marian was sitting there with tears in her eyes.

'It was lovely,' she said. 'I could believe it all.'

Her glance slipped to their glasses as if to check that those stupid swizzle sticks were still properly in place. They were. Goodness, what did she expect? Marian leaned forward on her stool and gave Harry a soft kiss on the lips. 'There are so many levels to your story-telling, Harry. I'm not absolutely sure which world I'm in.'

'I feel like that every day,' Harry replied. 'It's normal for me to be thinking of my next story, or even the one after next, even while I'm busy writing the one in front of me. Sometimes I sit, gazing into space as if I'm in a trance. And maybe I am, for I'm flitting between one world and the next, each with its own crazy rules. Sometimes I become confused and unhappy if I can't resolve some tale but, at others, I just cannot stop the flow. When that happens, I feel no longer responsible; the story is writing itself. All I have to do is copy it down. I always felt like that about Tom Sharpe's *Porterhouse Blue*, by the way; talk about being on a roll! I so wish I had written that story.' He paused. 'Listen,' he continued, 'thank you so much for turning up to hear my little story. By responding to my out-take last week, you set me off again. You removed a block and I, for one, have had such fun over the past days.'

'And I thank you, Old Harald, for giving me an insight into another world. It's been a beautiful experience and I'm so glad to have met you.'

This could be the start of something…

'Let's go,' Harry said and took her hand as they walked out of the bar.

    Their empty glasses tilted and clinked behind them.
    'Cheers!' his said to hers.

VOICES

The Whole Story

'I keep hearing voices.'
'So do I'

Details

'Oh! Very funny.'

'Yes… well, it's good to be succinct. Suppose I were to give you the full monty. I dare say boredom would set in pretty damn quick.'

'You forget. I know the full monty.'

'Well, perhaps you've forgotten some of it. And anyway, it changes. I'm not at all sure I know it myself right now. You will probably have to help me.'

'Yes, yes. It's always like this. You are just using me as a sounding board – someone to bounce ideas off.'

'That's true but you enjoy it anyway. And you're not alone.'

'True enough, but then neither are you. So what's irritating you this time?'

'I don't know yet but I was wondering how closely related are day-dreaming and sleep-dreaming. I read somewhere that the dreams we have when we're asleep are somehow expressions of our brains' tidying up the day's work…'

'Who said so? That's a reasonable suggestion, no doubt, but I don't see how degrees in psychology or psychiatry make those interpretations more plausible than anything I might concoct for myself without qualifications. Sorry; anything you might concoct for yourself.'

'OK, OK, let's not squabble over ownership for heaven's sake. What's yours is mine; what's mine is yours after all.'

'Listen – I've just had a thought. How are you going to convey to the reader who's talking at any given point? Are we to have names?'

'I've thought of that. The publishers' rule is to start a new paragraph when anyone new speaks, so that alone will indicate when the speaker has changed.'

'But after only a few such new paragraphs, the reader might well be left confused unless he has been keeping a very close watch. And why should she?'

'You're being clever again but anyway, it surely isn't going to matter. We're all in this together, aren't we? Let's go along as we are for a bit and see how it all works out. I was talking about dreams. I guess the point is that I have no conscious control of a sleeping dream but do of a day dream. But I'm not absolutely sure. Remember that lovely dream I had once – but only once, dammit – about being seated right behind the orchestra at a classical music concert in the Royal Albert Hall? Bert's Joint, as we disrespectfully called the place in our student days. The advantage of being in those seats is that you can see every movement the conductor makes. With his baton, of course, but with his fingers, his eyes – indeed with his whole body.'

'And if I may interrupt your tale for a moment, there is some parallel, don't you think, between a conductor guiding his merry men and women, and your consciousness guiding the direction of your dream.'

'I like that thought but if you're going to interrupt at every turn, we'll never get through this.'

'Why is it important that we *do* get through this? Surely this is only turning out to be some sort of stream of consciousness.'

'No. It is, at least, a *guided* stream of consciousness.'

'Ah! But who's guiding it?'

'Well not you, obviously.'

'You can see how this is likely to turn out to be rather complicated, can't you?'

'Oh! Here we go, someone else has joined in.'

'There are no rules. As many as wish may put their oar in. Once you start this sort of thing, there's no controlling it.'

'Oh, yes there is. No control equals madness and we're not going there.'

'That's alright, we don't mind some control, but actually a complete lack of control does not necessarily mean madness at all. It can just be the start of a wonderful ride. Lie back and enjoy it.'

'Look, I'm going to get back to that dream in Bert's Joint. I was sitting behind the double basses, I remember, which meant that I heard a most unbalanced performance.'

'Performance of what?'

'I've forgotten now. It doesn't matter. Probably something by Elgar.

I do remember, though, that at one point where the basses were *tacet* for some while, one bass player leaned towards another and said – quite audibly to me, at any rate – "Lovely toon". Meanwhile however, the orchestra were weaving their magic and the conductor was swaying as he waved his stick… '

'The word is "baton". Use the proper word.'

'Why? You knew what I meant. Pedantry is not next to godliness, you know.'

'Actually I, for one, do think that it's better to use the correct word when you can. It makes for a better reading experience.'

'Oh! God, now a fourth has joined us. Friend of yours?'

'Sorry, pay no attention. He's like that. He means well and is no doubt correct, but he has rather little tolerance for the loose of tongue. Anyway, sorry. I was rather enjoying the swaying of the conductor.'

'Yes well – that conductor was making many movements and flashing his eyes and so on but the most remarkable thing about him was that the amplitude of his movements was really quite small. He hardly moved but what little movements he did make were immediately clear to the players – and even to me, a mere spectator. Ah! I've just remembered his name because that part of the dream was more a memory than some fiction. It was Sir Adrian Boult, one of the two most influential conductors of British orchestras in the early to mid-twentieth century, the other being the flamboyant Sir Thomas Beecham. Interesting, that – you couldn't imagine two more different characters but it would be unfair to venerate one over the other. Anyway, there I was watching the minuscule movements of Maestro Boult and being utterly rapt in the sensuousness of the music. And, as I say, my dream was essentially recollection of my watching an actual concert some time before.'

'So where does the idea of "control" come into that?'

'Well, initially, I would say that there was none – or that I experienced none – in that I was simply remembering a real concert. But after some while, because I was becoming emotionally involved in the music, as if I were bathing in the sound, I found that I could linger a bit on some notes or phrases. Obviously, I couldn't stop the music (maybe it's not obvious but it seemed so at the time), but I could pull the timing about a bit, as a harpsichord teacher of my acquaintance used to say.'

'What's all that about?'

'It's called agogic accentuation. When you press a key on a harpsichord, a vertical stick of wood or plastic, called a "jack", bearing a small plectrum of quill, or another kind of plastic, plucks the string. However, it makes no difference whether you press the key lightly or thump it with all your might, the resulting sound has exactly the same volume and character. So, unlike a piano for which the volume is intimately linked to your finger pressure and speed of strike, the player is unable to emphasise any note by variation of volume. Instead, harpsichord players mess about with their timing – only slightly – so as to produce little hesitations which draw attention to a note or to that place in the music. This pulling the timing about is called agogic accentuation.'

'Thank you for that learned discussion but we do appear to have moved away from the main story.'

'Well, you did interrupt. You could instead just have accepted what I said without comment.'

'I'm in no mood to accept anything you say without question.'

'OK, but then you will get the long-winded explanations.'

'*I* think they're interesting.'

'Oh, *you* again! Thanks for your support.'

'You're welcome.'

'Now where were we, for goodness' sake? Oh yes, I was talking about how I was able to stretch the timing of the music to suit my enjoyment. As I said, like soaking in a hot bath.'

'Clearly your dream had some hidden, or maybe only partly hidden, sexual content.'

'You know, it's perfectly possible to wallow in sound without getting a hard-on. Freud really did bugger up life's simple pleasures, it seems to me.'

'More likely that it was some misunderstanding acolytes of the Great Man who got it wrong.'

'How reasonable you are. I'll stick with my crude summary, thank you very much. Back to my dream, people. After a while, maybe it was after falling asleep completely, the dream changed somewhat. I was, I think, still in the Royal Albert Hall, and certainly sitting behind the orchestra as before, but this time there was no conductor in front – or more precisely, no formal conductor – and the orchestra was a jazz orchestra. Not band – orchestra. It was a sizeable group and it was playing big group stuff like Duke Ellington or Count Basie or Gil Evans pieces. This time, I was seated right behind the heavy brass section; trombones, a tuba, some horns. The trumpets were somewhat in front. The music was swing and it sure swung. There were question and answer parts from right and left in the orchestra which made the sound sway even more, for the swing was quite literally like a wave washing from one side of the stage to the other. The saxophones and a couple of clarinets were all on the other side of the stage so there was an oscillation between brass and reed, connected – or do I mean separated – by percussion in the middle. I could distinguish the riffs from each section quite clearly and listen as each took dominance in its turn. But then something quite wonderful began to happen. I found that I could influence the music. The whole thing. I wasn't conscious of any mechanism, of any movements on my part. But by some act of will, I made the music take different forms. There was no particular tune involved as far as I could tell, but I seemed to be composing on the spot. Just like a good jazz musician, I suppose. Except that I have no musical training of any kind. I tried to learn to play piano in later life and did, thereby, come to understand what a pianoforte really is, but overall, my attempts were pathetic. I have never read music and, indeed, that's what finally put the tin hat on my playing attempts. But there I was in my dream, composing, as it were, and the whole orchestra were doing my bidding. Understand me here; this wasn't a dream about control of a bunch of players. I actually heard the music, the exchange from one section of the orchestra to another, and I made it all happen. In my dream, the players were anonymous and didn't seem to matter; certainly not as individuals. I was playing the orchestra! I suddenly introduced a stop, a *fermata*, as the excitement reached a temporary climax, only to release it a second or two later with a thunderous explosion from the percussion section before allowing the music to dissolve into lyricism and to swing away in a slow waltz.'

'Yeah, we've heard that story before. You appear to have suckered yourself into it quite deeply.'

'Yes, I know. But it seemed as real as reality. And it turned out to be a waking dream. I was so engrossed in it all, that it took some time before I began to realise that I was actually beginning to wake up. Oh no, I thought! I don't want this to end. And I fought to stay inside the dream. But I couldn't help myself. Very slowly but quite inexorably, I slid from dream to wakefulness. I remembered it all so clearly until, as I awakened more thoroughly and morning reality claimed me, much of it began to fade. I fought and fought to hang onto it and, as you see, I *have* managed to retain something, but most of the detail of that marvellous, expansive experience has gone. I often have repeat dreams but not that one.'

'So you were able to control that dream, for a limited time at any rate, but was your control provided only by the fact that you were about to awaken? After all, your subconscious might have been aware of your impending wakefulness well before the idea revealed itself to your consciousness.'

'It seems that this element of split mentality which I am experiencing right now was also alive and well within the dream. One part of me was enjoying the dream and the music; and another, like an orchestral maestro, was overseeing and guiding. A little nudge here, a little nudge there. Perhaps there was a deeper – or do I mean higher – influence, like a feedback loop maybe, that guided the overseer by reference to the result?'

'Now this is beginning to feel like a hall of mirrors. You stand between two parallel mirrors and see your face, and behind it the back of your head, and behind that your face looking at the back of your head, and so on *ad infinitum.*'

'That idea isn't new either. It was explored in some deliriously funny scenes in that nineteen sixties film, *Last Year in Marienbad* in which one questioned whether you were experiencing a memory or an anticipation, or a memory of an anticipation or an anticipation of a memory, and on and on. We were shown the same scene over and over again but with minute changes. I'd never seen anything like that before or since.'

'What *I* remember about that film was the mesmerising swaying motion of the heroine as she sashayed along the promenade. Instead of swaying her hips from side to side, she seemed to rock them forwards and backwards as if insinuating herself into the future at each step.'

'Sex again.'

'Maybe. Oh, shut up. Back to dreams… '

'Oh! Must we?'

'Why not? I'm in the mood.'

'Maybe the reader isn't.'

'Well, she can always put the book down. Nothing is obligatory. I'm thinking about one of my recurrent dreams, one I've not had now for many years. But I do remember it and I did so enjoy it. It was also a dream in which I had a measure of control, not only within the dream itself but also in that I could often call it up, as it were, like an old friend. It concerns flying… '

'Not that old chestnut. Everybody seems to have a flying dream.'

'Maybe but I think mine might have a bit of a twist.'

'They all say that.'

'This doesn't begin with me flying in the clouds. It begins with my making very great efforts to get up off the ground. I arch my back (it seems, as if by instinct, that I must make my chest curve well out and my back concave), lean forwards until I'm almost falling over, and flap my arms. In some way, the tensions in arching my back continue throughout my whole body and it's only when I achieve this whole-body involvement, that I begin to rise. For a while, I somewhat frantically flap away just to maintain myself a metre or so above the ground. But soon, I seem to achieve a degree of confidence, of self-belief, and I can do it without straining any more. At that stage, I begin to soar. But when I find myself at, say, five or six metres above ground, I look down, get a little scared and tense up, with the result that I lose lift. I don't fall to earth but I struggle to maintain flight. I keep trying and learn not to fear flying, but to enjoy heights. Then it all becomes easy and I can effortlessly soar, bank, descend, ascend and turn as I will. That is to say: as I *will* it. The whole thing becomes an exquisite pleasure, and like the musical dream perhaps, I begin to wallow, to luxuriate in the air, in my new dimension. Friends and acquaintances in the dream look on with wonder, delight and, maybe, some envy.'

'Ah! That's the giveaway. You're seeking admiration!'

'That may be true to some extent although I wonder more whether I might be seeking gratitude.'

'Why gratitude?'

'Once again, you keep interrupting. Listen; wait. All will become clear.'

'Pompous pri—'

'It's true. It's who I am, but let me continue.'

'So there I am, flying like a bird, soaring, swirling in three dimensions. Friends and acquaintances watch and marvel. But it's not enough to be admired or simply gawped at. I want to teach them to do it too! Not because I want their gratitude – at least I hope not too much – but because I really want them to enjoy what I am enjoying.'

'You sure you're kosher? You're just in need of some admiration, gratitude and the odd dollop of hero-worship.'

'Oh do shut up. I really don't think that is fair or true. I just want to share. Maybe I want to have fun sharing, though. But that's no sin, surely?'

'Why are you so preoccupied with sin? We all sin from time to time. Why do you believe you should be exempt? Or maybe you can't live with yourself? Is that it? Can't stand the guilt?'

'I'm sorry, I just used the word. It's convenient, that's all. I'm going back to my tale. In my dream, I spend a lot of time showing people how to fly. "Arch your back; make your chest stick out. Flap your arms. Believe. Believe". And I make the movements for them, over and over again. They copy. Some with silly grins on their faces. Of course, they'll never fly. But others with earnest eyes do try, and try again. They flap furiously and jump up into the air. And come back to earth immediately. It is so frustrating. Nobody else can do it. It seems that even believing in themselves isn't enough. Clearly, I have the gift. Where from? Why me? I just don't know. I get absolutely no satisfaction in being the only one, for I would dearly love to have fun and games with my friends in the air. But it's clear that it will not happen. The story's the same no matter how many times I have the dream. Despite all this, I crave to experience that dream again and again. The joy of flying is just so beautiful. Believe me.'

'Obviously, you were a bird in an earlier life.'

'Or you will be in the next!'

Cross Currents

'My turn – sorry. While you have been getting so hot and bothered, I've been somewhere else.'

'That implies that we can think about more than one thing at a time.'

'Nothing new there. What about the musicians you manipulate so cleverly? No, it's just that I've heard it all before and even I am getting bored with the subject, so while you were amusing your imaginary audience, I have been scraping my own barrel.'

'And?'

'You mentioned how comparisons between Beecham and Boult might be invidious. You talked about how one should revere these two musical giants equally.'

'Do you disagree?'

'Not at all. But my focus rather is on the word "revere". I would argue that such sentiments might be rightly linked with effort and achievement rather than with subject. We tend, don't we, to hold creators in the highest esteem: composers, writers, scientists, doctors, artists of one kind or another. But what about those whose strengths lie elsewhere: making things, building (as opposed to designing), running things like organisations or families. Surely what matters is whether a job is well done – maybe even whether there has been a good attempt at something.'

'Sounds patronising to me.'

'Yes, but that might be because of my language.'

'Always a problem with you, of course.'

'Thank you.'

'Always welcome.'

'Give it a rest you two! You are padding – looking for a way forward.'

'And thank you. Sometimes, that's necessary. And it acts as a kind of spacer or separator.'

'Look – getting back to the point. I don't feel that I'm patronising when I make a fuss over how well some tradesman or other does his job – her job. It may well be that there is little originality in the task but that doesn't mean you would tolerate a sloppy job. And, not only do I appreciate the result, I also quite genuinely admire seeing it accomplished – to watch the application of care and attention as well as the necessary skill. It might be argued that the fitting of a door, for example, is hardly as creative as the designing of a building; or as important as some piece of delicate surgery, maybe. And, in some respects that may be so. Certainly, there will be many more people able to hang a door than to perform transplant surgery. No doubt their respective salaries reflect that. But I still admire – I still revere – the artisan. Quite possibly as much as the professional. Maybe I am just saying that I respect the doing of a job well and with care. I mean, crikey! I admire many sportsmen – and women – I see on the telly I genuinely admire their skill and dedication. Yet I have little interest in sport, *per se.*'

'Sounds like the gentleman protests too much.'

'Yes, I know but I'd hate a world where only professionals matter.'

'Maybe you think you cannot compete sufficiently well.'

'Could be. But I don't think that invalidates my argument.'

'Not so much an argument – more some kind of cry for form and help, I think.'

'May I interject here? What about the many of us who don't try too hard because we find sufficient reward from doing something just well enough to get by? Why is it necessary to be the best at something, even if – or maybe, even not – it's an important cog in life's wheel? Such people may be very happy like that and providing for themselves and their families as we are all bidden by our betters.'

'He has a point. What's matter with a little sin, now and again? Why *must* we always try so hard?'

'I don't know. I don't know quite how to answer that. I do know that *I* must try. Always.'

'How often do you see folk who don't do their utmost – maybe at anything, I don't know – who seem blissfully happy?'

'And, for sure, they won't be interested in what you are saying right now.'

'Actually, that may not be true. I know folk who take an interest in the most amazing variety of subjects and people and yet have no intention of striving themselves. Nor do they feel an iota of guilt about that. And, dammit, they are happy!'

'Happiness isn't the be all and end of life.'

'Neither are striving, being perfect or being holy.'

'Me again…'

'Who's me?'

'Who cares?'

'Go on, "me again".'

'*Now* who's getting in on the act? This is really becoming impossibly complicated. It would seem that each side has several accomplices.'

'No sides here, mate. We're all one, remember!'

'I was trying to say something but now I've forgotten what it was.'

'Happens to *me* all the time.'

'Oh! I remember. The word we need in all this, surely, is category. Beecham and Boult were magnificent maestros. Da Vinci and Einstein were magnificent intellects. Olivier, Gielgud and Richardson were magnificent actors. Bill Davies and Geoff Mantel were magnificent tradesmen…'

'Never 'eard of them.'

'No and that's the point. The snobbery of our culture means that people like that are not heard of.'

'But aren't intellects, artists and thinkers worth more than artisans? I mean, come on. This is just between you and me.'

'And me.'

'And me.'

'And me…'

'I don't think so. We need all of them. And for all the obvious reasons, there will always be more artisans than intellectuals. Equally, there will always be even more of those who don't wish to strive but simply to enjoy.'

'So we just patronisingly put up with them?'

'No. They too are quite justifiably part of the landscape and are necessary for our species. It's only in science fiction that societies develop in such a way as to remove the weak, the hangers-on and, the category which is rarely mentioned, the floaters, shall we say – those who are content to float along with the tide. Who are we to deny them? For those who believe in the supernatural, I guess we might say that they are all God's creatures. Even totalitarian societies recognise what they like to call the "proles".'

'So what has been the point of the last section of this ramble?'

'I think it has just been a clearing of the throat. A reminder not to get above one's self. I will always try hard in everything *I* do. I can't really help it. But that is no reason to demand that others do the same. It would be disingenuous of me to say that I see the floaters in the same way that I see the geniuses, but that is no more than a statement of my psychology, of my conceit. We all choose our friends according to our lights.'

'And I remind you that the word "lights" refers to certain parts of our innards rather than to those bright things screwed into the ceiling.'

'Yes.'

Impulse to Join

'Is that it, then? Have you got it out of your system now?'

'Not quite. I've talked about how one can admire people in all walks of life but that doesn't mean, of course, that everyone is admirable. There are those who interfere in others' happiness by carelessness or by deliberate bastardry. I'm talking about criminals or those who, in my opinion, should be classified as criminals.'

'Stick 'em in clink. Simple.'

'Well it's not so simple. First there have to be rules, conventions and laws. It's obviously best if society – whatever exactly that means, because it probably only means those with power or those who, at some time in history, had power – can agree about what is acceptable and unacceptable behaviour and then expect people to conform. Much of that comes with mother's milk in that so much depends upon the quality of one's upbringing. Trouble there, is that some parents are products of bad upbringing themselves – and so on through the generations. While all that makes bad behaviour understandable, it doesn't make it acceptable. And take that word literally. Acceptable equals able to accept, and probably willingness to accept. So much, maybe, for conventions. After that we have rules and laws. There are probably differences between the two and my erstwhile lawyer friends would, no doubt, expand on them for hours.'

'I remember one such gleefully telling me a joke about his colleagues.'

'How did that go again?'

'Imagine a charabanc completely filled with lawyers – well almost filled, because there is one empty seat. And that charabanc is motoring down some zig-zag road along the cliffs of the Mediterranean coast, let us say. It's a very steep drive with lots of hairpin bends. Well, there comes a terrible accident; the bus careers off the road and falls over the cliff onto the rocks below. Everyone on board is killed. "How would you describe that situation most succinctly"? asked my lawyer friend. I look blank. "A missed opportunity"! He laughs gleefully.'

'Like Jews or the Irish, the best jokes come from within the group.'

'So sorry, I interrupted your tale of woe. Do carry on'.

'Well, I was trying to get to the question of what society is to do with those who break the rules. If their misdemeanours are small, we might pull a face as it were, or indeed, avert our face; but what if they are more serious? What if someone commits what society has deemed to be a crime?'

'We punish them, of course. Fine them or lock 'em up, or both.'

'Who gives us the right to do such a thing? Even for believers – Christians anyway – God wagged her finger and said "Vengeance is Mine". And, for non-believers like me – sorry, us – whence cometh the injunction?'

'From the law.'

'Oh! Come on. Let's not get into a circular argument. What is the basis, the origin, of any law? Surely it's no more than the expression of the power held by one or more people.'

'And where does their power come from?'

'The short answer is from history. Maybe some king uttered his fiat. Maybe some powerful group of lords issued a decree. More recently, a law might have been declared and agreed to by some elected body – probably a parliament.'

'I'm not happy about having to do what some long-dead king wanted, but laws passed by parliament have the authority of the people, surely.'

'By which you must mean, by the power of the people. The diktat of the masses. Surely that's not a good *moral* basis?'

'I suppose it was inevitable that *that* word should show up.'

'I presume that "moral" means a rule or law propounded by some religious authority.'

'And I would ask the same question: whence cometh that authority? I think the answer is much the same as I gave just now. It's simply a form of bullying by whomever had power at the time that the moral emerged.'

'*I* don't like that; therefore *you* will not do it.'

'Exactly.'

'OK. So what are we to do with people who break the law, who do unacceptable things?'

'We put 'em in clink or fine them, or both.'

'But you just said… '

'What I hadn't got around to is the resulting effect incarceration of offenders can have on us. I don't like the smugness that can result by our having put some bastard away. "He did the crime; he should do the time". I would prefer a little more humility. "There, but for the grace of God, go I".'

'You don't believe in God.'

'No, but the sentiment seems fine to me.'

'Is that what crime and punishment comes down to, then? Sentiment?'

'No; well, maybe. Maybe it comes down to sorrow. My bottom line is that we have no *right* to punish people; but we have the *necessity* to do so. We can't ignore serious transgression of our laws because otherwise our society would fall apart. Sure, we are applying the power of society – whenever and wherever that arose – to *maintain* our way of life. So we need to lock serious offenders up. But we should not feel righteous about it. We have the power and we are going to exercise that power. So look out criminals; we will incarcerate you. But with regret and sorrow. Maybe in centuries to come, there may emerge a better way. Or maybe, for reasons not yet apparent, people will refrain from crime.'

'How about refraining from sin?'

'Don't be silly. Far too difficult.'

'Are you done yet? I feel that it's time for a drink.'

'You have persuaded me.'

'Easy pickings.'

'What about sex? You haven't expanded on that subject yet.'

'This was supposed to be a *short* story.'

EXPECTATIONS

The Tramp

'He was here again today. This time outside Martin's shoe shop. What sort of impression does that give? I mean, nobody wants to buy from a shop which encourages people like that. Yesterday, he was in front of the kitchen utensil store. Exactly the same. He just stands there in his dirty, smelly clothes. He's dressed fit for deep mid-winter in Siberia rather than for the balmy breezes of the Mall. And what's that in his hand? It's the same every day. It looks like a bunch of newspapers wrapped up with a piece of string. He's like a walking trash can, for God's sake. It's not right. Something should be done about it. We pay rates don't we? We pay rents – bloody high ones at that – so what do we get for them? He's keeping custom away, that's what. Someone should do something about it.'

How many more days must I listen to this? "Someone", that is someone *else*, should do something. "We pay rates, we pay rents." Sure you do, just like everybody does. For your rates, you get exactly what everyone else gets – your garbage cleared, the streets cleaned and the threat of a rates rise. So what makes *you* so special? For your rent, you get an agreed floor area and services, same as everybody else. Nobody is picking on *you*. Now you've called the cops. Several times, I am given to understand. I know this because the cops have called me, as manager of the Mall. I have so little to do each day, that I am to welcome a friendly call from police headquarters? They have asked me what it's all about. What is this "it" for God's sake? I tell them I don't know. So they tell me to call them when I find out. What am I to do? Is it so bad for some guy to be poorly dressed and carry a newspaper? We all start with nothing, don't we? Whatever happened to "live and let live"?

It's time; I'm going for a coffee.

Not that simple. I always enjoy a coffee from the café in the open part of the mall. That way I can see what's going down. And I get to meet with some of my friends and I have to admit Cleo makes a good cup there. Nothing's perfect in life though. If there are problems I get harangued in my break. Am I not entitled to my break in peace like everyone else? Benny from the chocolate shop has buttonholed me. He wants to talk about the tramp.

'What is it with this tramp, Benny?' I ask. 'Surely we can live with some guy wandering around? I haven't heard that he's hurt anyone.'

'You should go for a walk around the place and see for yourself, Mike,' he urges. 'You would see how customers walk around him and look at him.'

'How do they look at him, Benny? With hate? With fear in their eyes? How?' I mean, isn't this all getting out of hand? You know, Benny's a nice guy. He's fair. I don't expect this from him. My bet is he was put up to seeing me by some of the other tenants.

'I would say people are embarrassed,' he replied. 'It's not right that customers should be embarrassed. It's not good for business, Mike. We don't expect people to behave like this.'

The customers or the tramp, I was tempted to ask but held my tongue. 'Seems to me that what's wrong is people's expectations.'

'You could be right, Mike, but you can't change people.'

Exactly, Benny, but that cuts both ways. Again, I said nothing. 'OK, Benny, I'll go walkabout. At this stage, though, all I intend to do is see for myself. I have no intention of rushing to judgement over this. Tell the others.' I finished.

So I went for a little walk. The mall is quite large and it took me some while to spot the tramp. I kept well out of the way and observed him for a while. He was a tall bloke, probably over six foot in old money, and basically quite handsome. He stooped a little. I would guess he was in his mid-sixties. His grey-to-white hair was unkempt but it didn't look dirty or greasy to me and he seemed to have had a shave but probably not today. He was wearing a thick, long overcoat which was worn and tatty but not, I would guess, particularly dirty. It was the coat of someone who had seen better days. The same could be said of his shoes. They were down at heel, clean enough though unpolished. From his left hand hung a bundle of newspapers, I would guess, tied up with string. It was an untidy-looking bundle. He was standing in front of a gents' outfitter. I had to admit that he was no advertisement for the establishment behind him. He hardly moved. Occasionally one step to the left, one step back; but that was about it. It certainly looked as if he'd been there for some time and it seemed that he had little intention of moving on any time soon.

The mall was not especially busy at that time in the morning but it wasn't deserted either. People were walking past, mostly intent on some errand or other. There weren't too many casual shoppers, randomly looking in shop windows. I continued to watch from a distance. A couple came up to the outfitter's window at a lazy pace and began looking at what was on offer. They didn't seem to mind the presence of the tramp, though. In fact, they hardly seemed to notice him. But they didn't enter the shop either but that could easily be because they saw nothing to tempt them. It all looked totally innocent to me. I began to walk around myself and look in various shop windows as inconspicuously as I could. I walked right past the tramp before stopping again at a suitably innocent vantage point. He didn't notice me. Actually, he didn't seem to notice anyone. Some more window-shoppers came up to the outfitters, a couple again. The man drew his partner's attention to something but she studiously avoided coming anywhere close to the tramp. Indeed, she somewhat pointedly drew her partner's attention to him. The tramp seemed not to notice them. The woman drew her man away from the shop and they continued their exploration of what the mall has to offer elsewhere. Of course, it could be that they remained unimpressed with what they had seen in the window. I couldn't tell.

I grew bored with watching after a while and decided to go for a stroll to stretch my legs. As I moved off, Pauline from the florist's shop dashed out and more or less pulled me into her den.

'You've been watching him, haven't you?' she said but before I could answer, continued. 'You see what it's like. He's been standing there for half an hour at least. Hardly moves. And what's with them papers? This is supposed to be a high class mall. You don't expect to see dirty tramps like that hanging around.'

'He doesn't actually look dirty to me, Pauline. He's a bit scruffy and could do with a shave, maybe.'

'Why doesn't he move?' she asked, shifting her line of attack somewhat.

'No idea, Pauline,' I replied. 'I'm going away for a while. Let's see where he is when I return.' I needed to pee anyway so I felt that I was using my time well as I took off. Actually, I decided then to pop back to my office for a while. I had some boring paperwork to do. I thought I'd get through that before venturing out again. When I finally decided to go walking once more, nearly an hour had slipped away.

I got back to the vicinity of the outfitters, and found that the tramp had gone. I wasn't sure whether to feel disappointed or not. Pauline saw me and popped out of her den.

'He left about ten minutes ago, 'she said. 'He went off in the direction of the food court.'

I thanked her and started for that direction too. She was quite right. I spotted him in the food court queueing at the sandwich bar. There were a couple of people ahead of him in the queue but nobody behind. I watched from a safe distance. Nobody joined the queue behind him. I thought someone was about to do so but she seemed to change her mind at the last moment and looked for a different food outlet. It did seem as if she were avoiding the tramp but I couldn't be absolutely sure. These things can be so subtle. The tramp ordered and paid for his meal and took it to a nearby vacant table. I continued watching. The adjacent tables remained unoccupied for some time, longer than I would have expected really, but in due course, some man came up and took a seat at the next table. Clearly everybody didn't feel the same way – or notice him, perhaps. The tramp spoke to nobody nor did he make eye contact. He simply sat and ate, minding his own business. He got up after some while and moved off. A young couple moved to another table close to where he had been sitting. The tramp returned rather soon, however, carrying a cup of tea and sat down again at the same table. His newspaper bundle hadn't left his spare hand at any time. The newcomer couple looked at the tramp rather closely, clearly didn't like what they saw, got up and carried their food off to another table some way off.

I decided that I had to find out if this joker smelled offensive in any way so I bought myself a cup of tea and sat down at the table just vacated by the young couple. The tramp seemed not to notice either the departure of the couple or my arrival. It must have looked pretty peculiar as I leaned forward from time to time, pretending to fasten my shoe lace on one occasion, or picking up a button on another, as I tried hard to sniff the air. I smelt nothing untoward. Close up, I had to admit, the tramp presented a somewhat daunting appearance and his bundle of papers did seem messy. But that was all there was to it. I took my time drinking my tea and waited for him to leave. That was beginning to take forever so I changed plan and took off myself but not too far. I had become intrigued with this fellow and wanted to observe him some more. I found myself a discreet spot some way away and waited for him to leave the food hall.

I had to wait for ages before he picked up his bundle and moved off. I was curious as to whether he would now leave the mall or find another place to stand around. He walked fairly slowly. It wasn't the shuffle of an old man, though – simply a slow amble. He didn't look in any shop windows as he went along. He just walked. He came across a toilet and went in. I wondered for a moment whether this had been the whole point of his day; whether he was up to no good in there. But I didn't follow him in for, although he'd shown no sign of seeing me in the food court, I didn't want to take the risk of being accused of following him. I needn't have worried. He came out of the toilet after only a few moments and other people had been coming and going during that time without any sign of anything amiss. Thank God for that, I thought, for I really didn't fancy accosting a pervert or worse.

The tramp continued on his way, at the same measured pace. It looked like he might be leaving the mall completely. But no! Suddenly – if coming to a halt from a slow walk can ever be described in that way – he stopped outside another shop. This time, it was a bookstore. He didn't bother to look in the window and I formed the impression that he had absolutely no idea of what shop he had stopped in front of. He had simply stopped. And there he began another vigil, as it were. Standing still, but for an occasional shuffle, looking blankly out at, or was it through, the passing shoppers, newspaper bundle in hand. I was about to move off and go back to the office for my sandwiches when the head seller from the bookstore came out of his shop and accosted the tramp. I couldn't hear what was said but he seemed very angry and was gesticulating for the tramp to leave. The tramp looked at the shopkeeper very calmly and said a few words. These seemed to inflame the shopkeeper who began to push the tramp. That was something I could not tolerate, of course, and I began walking briskly from my observation post towards them but well before I reached the scene, the tramp turned around and began walking away. By the time I got there, the shopkeeper was standing alone with a rather red face.

'What was all that about, Nick?' I asked.

'It's that bloody tramp again. He stands outside my store for hours. Never moves. Puts customers off. I've had enough, Mike. We don't expect riffraff like that in this mall. This is a high-class mall. After all, we pay enough to retail here.'

'What did he say to you just now?' I asked.

'The cheeky sod just told me that he was doing no harm. That he was minding his own business so why couldn't I mind mine. Well I am minding my business. I am looking after it. I am not happy, Mike. Something just must be done about that bugger. That means you, Mike. Sorry but that's your job. What are you going to do?'

'Well, I hear what you're saying, Nick, and I have spent some time today watching and looking for myself. I'm going back to my office for a nice long think but I would really appreciate your behaving yourself in the meantime. I'll do something, Nick, but not in the heat of the moment.' At that, I left for my office and a bit of peace before the coming battle, whatever that might turn out to be.

Pow Wow

Good to sleep on things, don't you think? A little before my usual coffee break next morning, I left my office in search of the tramp. I realised, of course, that he might not come into the mall that day but I had to see. I guessed that he might be found somewhere along a different "arm" of the mall from where he was lingering yesterday. It's quite far out that way but there was no sign of him. I thought I'd give it one more shot in the area he had frequented yesterday before I gave up and went for my morning coffee. Luck, it seems, was shining down on me for there he was, quite close in fact to my favourite café, standing with his bunch of newsprint near an isle outlet selling phone cases. Making sure not to be too aggressive by marching up to him, I nevertheless approached him directly. 'Good morning, sir,' I began. 'My name is Mike Bennington. I am the manager of this mall. May I offer you a cup of coffee in return for a short conversation?'

He redirected his gaze from the floor to my face and replied, with a somewhat quizzical expression, 'It's not every day that I get an offer like that. Thank you. I'd be glad to share a coffee with you.'

I was somewhat taken aback, for he spoke clearly and well, with an educated voice and was obviously a confident man. We strolled along to Cleo's café and sat down.

'What would you like?' I asked the tramp. He chose a flat white, as did I. 'May I ask your name, sir?' I asked.

'Charles Griffin,' he replied. He wasted no time. 'You look like a man with a problem,' he continued. I had thought it was me conducting this interview.

'Mr. Griffin,' I said, 'I don't know whether you are aware of the effect you are having on shopkeepers and shoppers in the mall.' I thought it best to get down to it straight away, especially in light of his forthrightness.

He gave a watery smile and said, 'I suppose you are talking about that little contretemps outside the bookstore yesterday.'

'Well yes, in part,' I began.

He interrupted. 'I saw you there, observing me, of course. In fact you had been following me for much of the day.'

I was amazed. I thought that I had been so discreetI tried not to interfere with your – how can I say? Meandering, perhaps – and I certainly didn't want to impede you in any way.'

'Yet today, you have done so. Why is that?' he asked. He asked it in a perfectly polite way. I could take no offence.

It's not my way to prevaricate. 'Well, despite your manner of seeming to be half asleep, it's clear that you are fully aware of your surroundings, and that being so, you must have seen how several shoppers have avoided you, sometimes feeling obliged to go to another store. You must similarly be aware that several shopkeepers have been upset by your presence outside their businesses. Many have been to see me, as manager of the mall, to complain.'

'I've done nothing wrong. What have they said?' he asked.

I decided to be totally frank. 'They describe you as a smelly, dirty tramp in unsuitable clothes, carrying a trash-can of newspapers around with you.'

'My my, you are frank!' said Griffin.

'I am so because your question was frank. It seemed to me that you would prefer an honest conversation,' I replied.

'I do, and I thank you for it,' he said.

'Then do you understand the concerns which my tenants have expressed?' I asked.

'Not really. First – I'm not dirty, nor are my clothes. Surely you can see that. Secondly, I don't believe that I exude an offensive smell. By the way, I am aware that you examined that yourself yesterday.'

I felt duly embarrassed by this last remark. 'Yes, I'm sorry, but I felt I had to check that for myself. I don't take another's word in any complaint.'

'I understand, and it is better that way. So tell me: do you find me dirty or smelly? Do my clothes seem dirty to you?'

'No to all three. Some would find you untidy but so what? That's undoubtedly your business.' I mean, I have always prided myself on straight speaking. What else could I say?

'You mentioned my bundle of papers. Actually, they are not newspapers but a complete and unique set of papers from my former career which are precious to me. Not that that's anybody's business, by the way. I want to keep them safe.'

'Why do you just wander about and hang about outside shops all day?' I asked.

'Ah! I think we're getting close to the nub of the matter,' Griffin said. 'Again, it's really nobody else's business but you have been fair and honest so I will tell you. I am retired. I am without a wife or children; in short, I am alone in the world. But I do get lonely and it helps just to be amongst people scurrying back and forth doing their shopping or whatever. I have never been much good with people. I don't like to start conversations. Indeed, this is probably the longest conversation I have had with anyone in years. I mean no harm. I am just observing the world go round. I do realise that this upsets some folk but that was never my intention. I just want a quiet life.' He stopped talking, and for once, looked me straight in the eyes. His showed both hurt and sadness.

I wasn't enjoying my task one little bit but I had to achieve something. 'Mr. Griffin,' I began, 'I would much prefer not to have had this conversation with you although I must say how much I appreciate your being so honest and clear. I believe everything you have said and I, for one, do not find you offensive in any way. You do set a sad figure who is difficult to ignore. You are not the sort of person one expects to find in this sort of mall. The mall is private property and it is perfectly within my power to insist that you leave and not return. I would be doing so on behalf of the several shopkeepers who have complained of your presence to me – and also on behalf of those shoppers who have been similarly offended by you, even though they have not complained directly – to anyone, so far as I know. I do have that authority, Mr. Griffin.'

'I know,' he said. 'I was a lawyer – not a barrister – in my former life so I do understand your position completely.'

'Mr. Griffin,' I continued, 'I don't want to do any such thing. As I say, you don't offend or upset me in any way personally but I must keep my tenants sweet. I wonder if I might instead *ask* you not to visit the mall and to linger as you have been doing, *as a personal favour to me?*'

That was all it took.

He inclined his head and looked at his feet. 'Yes. I'll do as you ask.'

I have never felt such a jerk ever before or since.

'Thank you. Please come in from time to time, however, and share a coffee with me. Here's my card. You can phone me any time.'

Griffin took the card and nodded but said nothing more. I never saw him again.

A Present

I did hear from him, however. It was several months later that a small parcel appeared in my in-tray. It was neatly wrapped in brown paper but had clearly been delivered by hand. Inside was a brief note:

For Mike Bennington. Maybe this serves as an avatar for me. Charles Griffin.

He had sent me what seemed to be a miniature piano or other keyboard instrument. Certainly, it was in the form of such. All told, it was about ten centimetres across and perhaps four deep. It seemed to be made of wood and it had a short keyboard – less than an octave – with keys apparently made of ivory and ebony. As I moved the instrument around, the sensitive keys moved a little and I could hear soft sounds as if an internal mechanism were attempting to strike strings. Unfortunately, the whole thing was encased in strong Perspex or such. I presumed that it was some form of packing or travel protection and I looked for some point of attachment which I could unfasten. But there was none. The strong plastic encircled the instrument without break or seam and appeared to be firmly attached to everything except the keys, which was why they were able to move, of course. After more lengthy examination, it became apparent that the plastic cover was an integral part of the thing. I had been sent a solid moulded artefact with internal moving parts which tempted one to think could be manipulated from outside, but actually, could not.

What was the point of such an object? What was its purpose? Because of its appearance as a miniature keyboard instrument, one might assert that it was not fit for purpose. Whose purpose? It just didn't do things as one would expect. I must say that I found it rather irritating. That made me think.

A Wider Audience

I also heard *about* Griffin. That was some months later when his photograph appeared in our local newspaper. Mind you, he was looking decidedly the worse for wear. It seemed that he had been set upon in the street – not too far from the mall, actually – by some young thugs. A short article accompanying the photograph described how a "Mr. Charles Griffin (66)" was attacked by three or four youths. A passer-by had managed to apprehend one of the culprits who was later taken to the police station and, with his associates, was charged with actual bodily harm. Mr. Griffin was taken to hospital for observation but discharged soon thereafter. Mr. Jacob Unswell, an onlooker at the time of the assault, told their reporter that Mr. Griffin had regularly been seen standing outside the Griswell Street bus station. "He seemed like a typical sort of tramp to me, shabby and greasy, wearing a thick, long coat and carrying a bundle of newspapers or something. I heard someone say that he had upset some of the people queueing for their bus. One of the youths who beat him up said that he was a pervert, I think."

    The short report ended by saying that the assault case was scheduled for trial in eight weeks' time. No address had been given for Griffin. That was right and proper, of course, but it meant that I couldn't contact him to offer my sympathy. I really wanted to do that.

    I had expected that we would hear no more about it from that newspaper. After all, they need new stories every day to sell their rag. So it was with some surprise and concern when some days later, I came across two separate letters to the editor on the subject. Neither expressed any concern for Griffin or his injuries. Instead, they railed on about the increasing number of vagrants in our town – of how this writer had actually seen this tramp loitering; loitering with intent, the writer said, omitting, however, to name the intent. One writer suggested – he didn't actually come out and say, however, for no newspaper would have allowed it, surely – that the tramp was accosting young people as they queued for transport. And they made clear that they were not just talking about begging for cash. I thought these letters were utterly disgusting.

Two days later, however, there appeared a third letter on the subject which described how Griffin used to loiter in our mall.

"Many people were offended by his appearance and by the fact that he would just stand in one place for what seemed like hours. But,' said the writer, 'there was never any complaint about his behaviour towards others in the mall. He is probably just a lonely old man who deserves to be left in peace. He certainly does not deserve to be beaten up in the street and vilified by ignorant and prejudiced onlookers. This is the worst example of 'street justice' I've ever seen. It seems to me that thugs who beat him up in print are no better than the thugs who beat him up in the street." The letter was signed by Benjamin Harris.

'Benny!' I almost shouted as I read this wonderful defence of Charles Griffin. Benny, my coffee mate. I always thought of him as a fair man. Now he was sticking his neck out in the name of fairness. But matters didn't end there. How could they? The next day saw a rebuttal by one of the earlier letter-writers. He objected to being called a "thug". He hadn't beaten up the old man. He was just making fair comment about the state of our streets.

I knew I shouldn't have joined in on all this but I just couldn't help myself. After all, Benny had shown his fairness and might well cop some flak from other tenants in the mall. I had to show some support for the man. My letter appeared in the paper the very next day.

I referred to the last writer who had bemoaned the state of our streets. "One might suppose from your correspondent's letter that our streets are infested with dirty tramps assailing passers-by morning, noon and night. This affair concerns just one old man who has not been shown to interfere with anybody at any time. He is the victim here. Yes, he has been seen in the mall on several occasions and complaints have been made about him. As manager of the mall, I spent some time observing his behaviour closely. I never once observed him showing disrespect to anyone. He is neither dirty nor smelly. He is just a lonely bloke who wants to be left in peace. In my capacity as spokesman for the retailers in the mall, I felt obliged to ask him not to come there again. He agreed not to do so and he has kept his word." I finished my letter saying, "I bitterly regret asking

Mr. Griffin to leave. He is a gentleman who deserves peace and respect. And the rest of us deserve a newspaper which refuses to print the mindless filth of blind prejudice."

I thought that that should sink me without trace. I began thinking about where I might find a new job.

The editor, however, was obviously enjoying the whole thing. He had no intention of closing down correspondence on this topic. Most notably, two further letters appeared the next day, both saying roughly the same thing. Indeed, they were so similar in tone, at least, that I suspect collusion between the authors. No matter. The authors identified themselves as shopkeepers in the mall and, in essence, they supported what Benny and I had written. To my astonishment and delight, they agreed that Griffin had never done any harm and that they were sorry ever to have complained to me about him in the first place. They spoiled their case a bit when they added, "We were only trying to protect our customers from what *they* saw as a threat." That was cheap. But at least they had come out on the side of the angels. Of course they were hypocrites but, at least, they had made a proper *public* stand. And that had taken some courage, I would say. Actually, I did say it for I went round to see them as soon as I had seen their letters and I told them so. So now we were all a bunch of hypocrites, I suppose. But something is always better than nothing, don't you think?

So it's all about fitting in, conforming, satisfying others' expectations. I received a short note the other day from Charles Griffin.

"I did not like the publicity one bit but I do thank you for your fair play."

RANT

My Musical Groin

Excitement comes in many ways, does it not? Who would have foretold in the 1980s that in only thirty-odd years, one might enjoy the frisson of a burbling mobile phone stuffed down your pants? I'm driving along with my phone in my trouser pocket, out of harm's way so that I will not be tempted to answer any calls whilst driving, when, all of a sudden, as they used to say in calmer times, my device receives yet another riveting notification that the prince and his wife dressed today in matching colours or maybe, that herewith are thirteen new recipes for spiced pumpkin or some similar delicacy beloved by our porcine friends.

I could have turned the phone to "mute" of course, but then follows the bind of deciding when to unmute the blasted thing and, even worse, forgetting which state you left it in. You might miss an important phone call. Or it might have been a robocall; then you would have forgone the delights of stringing along the lady ("Nichole", she announces. She doesn't know that my late friend's basset hound was called Nichole; and she stank, by the way) for as long as you can bear or afford before revealing to her her new direction in life. Now then – no need to feel guilty. After all, everyone needs a job; but why choose to be a criminal? She feels no shame in wasting your time with the daily warnings of imminent disconnection from the Web. It wouldn't be so bad if the lies varied. At least there would be some entertainment value in the scam. Wait, though. Isn't it *your* fault for not checking the displayed number before answering? That, at least, is one up on the old telephones. Well no! Of course, because who has the right to tell you what to do with your own gadgets? And by the way, when exactly did "gadget" get replaced by "device"? Of course! It was about the time that "program" (computer program, that is) got replaced by "app", which is short for application. Someone obviously thought that "program" sounded a bit technical. How bloody patronising.

And, while I'm on about language, who sanctioned the loss of the adverb? Who accepted the reply to "How are you" as "Good" so inviting the response, "I was enquiring after your health, not your morals"? Who first decided that countable things are no longer countable? You know – as in, "The *amount* of people who can speak good English… " instead of "The *number* of people who are just too ignorant or lazy to get it right… "

"Now, now" I hear, "Just who are you to be so patronising? After all, such changes simplify the language so that foreigners can master English more easily. You should be pleased that English has assumed primacy throughout the world". Well, of course I am, for otherwise I might have to learn other languages myself. So I'm hypocritical, or selfish, probably both. But that is no reason to desecrate our wonderful language. I am told, by those who know better than me, that our language is wonderful precisely because it can accommodate so many changes and double meanings. Nevertheless, any Frenchman would understand and applaud my protest. Mind you, one should be careful in assuming one knows how a whole foreign population might respond. I do so remember a lunch meeting with a charming French professor (of physics, as I recall, not that that is of any relevance at all) to whom I confessed my admiration for his country. He replied that he felt a similar admiration for mine.

'I didn't express my admiration merely to evince yours,' I said.

'But I meant every word,' he insisted. This, I had not expected.

'But what about the Frenchman's view on sex and love? On beauty and form?' I protested.

'Ah yes!' he conceded . 'But what about politics?'

We agreed to go through for lunch. Mind you, all that was pre-Brexit.

But I digress. And why shouldn't I? This is *my* story, tale, moan, after all. I remember as a young kid, looking forward to reaching maturity at thirty or so, because youngsters would then show respect to me, their elder. I waited until I was forty, then fifty, before accepting that it was never going to happen. My dad's mantra had been something along the lines of 'The younger generation have never had it so good; they show no respect, we had that years ago… *et cetera, et cetera.*' Now it's my turn. I garner the same success. But surely, capitulation is piss weak. If you have standards, fight for them. I will and I do. But I get tired, you know. Maybe I'll snuggle down under the bedclothes, raise the drawbridge and mind my own business. But how can I with that jingle in my groin? We have all been suckered by Silicon Valley and so we must take on the Great American Dream. Fight! Make money! Be successful! For *those* pioneers, these are all different facets of the same thing, of course. But not for me, dammit! Decency and gentleness are other aspects of the "good life", aren't they?

Today – but it could be any day – I received nine or ten emails offering to make me rich: by purchasing bitcoins; by shopping online at [fill in your own favourite stores]; by buying funeral insurance; by consulting Madame X, clairvoyant; by calling Susie, whore; by having my toenails polished. For Christ's sake, leave me alone! Don't call me; I'll call you. Have a nice day.

I remember when that vacuous phrase first came into common use, by the way. It was, surprise, surprise, in the United States, home of anything new and home to people ranging from crass, grasping, presidential fools to gentle, genteel, subtle mortals. On this occasion, it was a response by Groucho Marx to that farewell from a cab driver in the wee small hours.

'Have a nice day!' said the cabbie, as he drove away.

'Mind your own goddamn business. I'll have any sort of day I like!' replied Groucho.

See, I'm not the only one who moans and rants.

'Why can't a woman be more like a man?' wailed Professor Higgins. You can't disagree with that! But nor can you disagree with those who point out the obvious, either. That's the trouble with rants. You know you're being stupid but you can't stop. You have so much RIGHT on your side! And wrong. Why can't things be straightforward and simple?

Some Balance

I do like my smart phone really. It does all those extra things you like, including some you really believed you'd always wanted a phone to do. How nice to see a photo of your caller so that you can reply "Hi Judi" immediately without the need for, "Who is it? Say again; it's a bad line". How nice to be able to bring up a map of the place you're going to. What a godsend Google is! Three cheers for Wikipedia! How simplifying that it isn't spelt, Wikipaedia. See; my spell-check tells me it isn't! The on-line Oxford English Dictionary is so – so useful – isn't it? If only you weren't interrupted by those ads every time you consult it. Well pay for an ad-free app, for goodness' sake; cheapskate! And what about WhatsApp? I can phone across the world for nothing, or at least, nothing extra – and with a video link, if I want. That's something straight out of Marvel magazines *circa* 1970; or do I mean 1930? And I can use the phone camera to take photos and even movies! It's so easy to forget that it's supposed to be a phone!

In earlier life, as a scientist, I wrote many computer programs using Autocodes and Fortran. So it was with the confidence of a know-all expert that I foretold, back in the 1980s, that personal computers (which all the world knows as PCs) would never take off and the idea that in future one would see and use programs which use ninety-eight per cent or more of the computing power of your device merely to provide a pretty landscape and a touchy-feely user interface was quite utterly preposterous. It would never happen! By the way, with this track record, I regularly invest in lotteries. Don't forget, you cannot teach an old dog new tricks.

I still prefer to read books in hard copy; actually, given the choice, in hard back. I know full well that I am not alone in this but I warn with my wagging finger that it is entirely possible our kind will die out. I compromise, however, by using my online dictionary and translator (between strange, live or dead languages of which I know nothing) while reading my "real" book.

So far, I've not mentioned two other wonderful – or should that be wonderfully wasteful – attributes of our everyday devices. (In parenthesis, do you think that "device" might be derived from "devious vices" by any chance? I only ask.) I am thinking of newscasting and social media. It is newscasting which is by far the major culprit in vibrating my nether regions – of providing my groin with sensuous jingles. Someone, somewhere, has decided that I simply must hear about the three-day-old, inconsequential occurrence every bit as much as the latest horror story from anywhere in the world. A good friend of mine used to observe, 'A man's gotta have an occupation.' At least, selecting my stories of the day, which after all, is just what newspaper editors have done for years, can be an honourable pursuit, to be markedly differentiated from that selected by the Nicholes of this world. And anyway, I have considerable control over the matter as it is up to me to select or reject the dozens of different possible news sources. Of course, rather like my incessant punting on the lotteries, I find it difficult to resist the possibility that next time it might come up with a useful recipe or an interesting take on wormholes in outer space. No, I guess the real problem in all this is how easy it is to spend too much time with your head buried in your device instead of engaging with real life as it happens. Then again, your real life might be too boring to bear, too grey to bring colour to your cheeks. Escapism is all. Could time spent in this pursuit be grounds for divorce, I wonder?

Alright; I've held off long enough. Social media are what I'm on about. Should that be "is" these days? I'm not going for that. Or anti-social media, as I would prefer to call them. Many moons ago, when I was but a stripling, I hankered after the ability to hold forth to the general public when I felt aggrieved, annoyed, or just that way out. I fantasised interrupting radio broadcasts (this was way before the wonders of television) with my spicy wit, my *bon mot*, my gritty put-downs, my *really important* views. It never occurred to me that others may have harboured the same desire. Or that they may be numbered in their millions. Or that they would SHOUT. I have already confessed to my shortcomings in the area of fortune-telling so I can, at least, claim some degree of consistency. What has happened to us that we should stare at our devices to catch the merest whiff of the latest trivial notion? It seems that breaking wind is an act of creation worthy of a broadcast. My wife and I shared a lunch table with a good friend a couple of years ago in a pleasant, and quite busy, Japanese restaurant. As we exchanged news and views over sushi and tempura, a table nearby began to fill up with a party of about a dozen young men – mostly Japanese, we guessed, but I don't think that was in the least bit important – who took out their phones almost before their bums hit their seats. They didn't speak a word to each other, although their body language made clear that they were friends; indeed, no word was said throughout their whole meal except to order it. I've often wondered what they thought of us, assuming of course that they actually clocked us. Perhaps they wondered what on earth three obvious friends had left to talk about. Were we merely reciting old news? Simply brushing our egos to maintain artificial contact? That could be it because a lot of social intercourse involves just that. But if you find that altogether too trivial, too ritualistic, why meet up at all? Stay at home, or in your office, or on a park bench where you can masturbate your device to your heart's content. If you don't need anybody, you don't need anybody, for goodness' sake. I really have tried to see things from the "new" point of view but I can't. I don't like most "pop" music but I can imagine that I might. I remember my father's disparaging remarks about the popular music of my young day but I caught him whistling the odd "modern" tune nevertheless. But where's the point in gathering, only to ignore one another? Is it just to feel one another's presence? Could be – husbands and wives do that all the time. But they seem not to go out to do it. On second thoughts, maybe they do. Maybe that's the answer. Maybe those devices are a means by which young folk may transform into old without the need to pass through the years. I think I'll patent that thought.

Then came the phenomenon we call Donald Trump. His surname refers to the passage of air over warm faecal material, of course, but that might not be relevant. Suddenly, policy is made and announced *via* a tweet on a platform called Twitter. I realise that it's good to catch 'em young but is this not extreme? I rant on about it. You know that. But I do. And I have lost! Other world leaders (President Macron, for one) have joined in. Actually, the political power of the tweet was probably exploited first by Trump's favourite punch-bag, none other than Barack Obama and his team. You must remember; water runs downhill. So does piss, of course. Once again – I have lost! Get over it! Adjust. It's a brave new wassnim out there. (Dear Editor, please don't correct that word; my wife invented it and I like it. Tell your spellcheck that it's acceptable and it will never bother you again.) That's how to change reality, by God! Just type in the new version.

Must I Choose?

I'm a lost soul, aren't I? Between the devil and the deep blue sea. Between a rock and a hard place. Which do you prefer? I think I like the first; it has some poetry about it. Modern living means we don't have to get our hands dirty. So build with a large footprint; keep the garden to the size of a pocket handkerchief. Pave it with stones and artificial grass. If you mix in plastic blooms amongst your real plants, you can have colour all year round. Be a total expert. Do just your job, whatever it is, and buy in the rest. Why cook? Get take-aways. Then why bother with a kitchen and a cooker? A kettle and a microwave should cover all your needs. You like kids? Play with your brother's/sister's/friend's and give them back afterwards. You like pets? Install some soppy photographs; they don't need cleaning, feeding or being taken to the vet. Like travelling? Take a cruise. Everything is done for you, more or less. Wondering what's going on at home while you're away? Use the phone app to check your CCTV cameras. Defecation and urination are down to you, sorry.

Now look here, you think I'm over-blowing all this? Not so. You may not find people who subscribe to everything above, but you will find those who subscribe to some things – and to others not mentioned, as well. This brave new world was foreseen by many science fiction writers in the last century, of course. You don't have to follow the more bizarre sci-fi films. Just think of Arthur C. Clark's stories. His style was to anticipate the future but only by a small margin. His ideas were merely logical and informed extensions of what was around as he wrote. I intend no criticism here; he did it very well. But even he didn't anticipate much of what we have around us now. The changes have been enormous, and enormously swift. And there are many more immediately around the corner. There haven't been correspondingly swift changes in human nature, however, and probably most people wouldn't want there to be. This mismatch will grow ever more serious. There's enough time for silly old buggers like me to get by. I shall cark it before it all gets too serious,

I do believe, but I worry for my children's generation, and certainly for my grandchildren's. Yes! I am fully aware that the same sort of thing was said by my parent's generation, but this time it *is* different. And no! It's not good enough to say "They all say that" as this time it's different because the pace and nature of the changes are so great. We worry about climate change; and we should. But if the worst comes to the worst, we might be able to get ourselves out of the shit by manipulating the amount of sunshine the globe receives by placing silver shards in the stratosphere or something. What I'm on about, however, is likely to be a continuing tear in the human fabric, year on year, and I make no pretence of being able to offer any solutions. I shall retire into my pit, cover my eyes and keep warm but I'm well aware that will not make the whole thing go away.

Am I being dragged, kicking and screaming into the twenty-first century? How am I doing, I wonder? Who's doing the dragging? Well, maybe it's those children – and not just those with less than sixteen years under their belts – who make Hollywood explode. Look how many futuristic films go the rounds these days. Why so many? Obviously because they are so incredibly successful. Profits are measured in the billions of dollars. Billions! Does all this define our society? Rule by the base, the plebs, hoi polloi (not *the* hoi polloi, by the way, but why should anyone care any more when the amount of people using the definite article is so large?). Snob, elitist. Why is education so important? You can earn just as much without it – more, as like as not. So there's the bottom of the well – money. It always was, wasn't it?

The final metric.

Sounds like the pop song from the eighties.

BROTHER, SISTER, HUSBAND, WIFE

PART 1
HONOR and ARNO

Putting on the Dog

On a pleasantly warm September day that year of 1896, many of nearly one hundred and twenty passengers were strolling on the deck of the *Juno,* which had steamed back and forth on the Baltic and North seas between Hull in England and Hamburg in Germany since 1888. While some eight hundred and fifty thousand souls called Hamburg home at that time, Hull could boast less than a quarter of that number but Hull, you know, was a far more important city in England then than it is now. After London and Liverpool, Hull was Britain's third port from which were exported coal and cotton, oil cake and flour, and to which were imported wool, wheat, petrol and wood. It was Britain's main fishing port and a major passenger gateway as well. So, as the nineteenth became the twentieth century, there were some rich people around. Certainly, there were plenty of poor ones too but the existence of the wealthy raised the quality of the amenities and reputation, both nationally and internationally, of that ancient city port. It was, perhaps, a more desirable destination at the end of the nineteenth century than it is now.

Frederick Baeber had spent nearly three months of the summer in Schleswig-Holstein, painting pictures and tracing his immediate forebears. While he kept body and soul together by his trade as a tailor, his great love and hobby was painting in oils. He was not good enough *yet*, he mused, to earn his keep from his painting alone but he was a first-rate amateur, specialising in rustic scenes which he painted with considerable subtlety in the impressionist style. He was a dapper fellow, smartly dressed that day in a warm tan suit, elegantly shaped, polished brown shoes, an informal but well-laundered soft cream shirt, and a large but limp, red and magenta bow tie. Frederick hoped that his attire neatly reflected the two sides of his life; perhaps he was a little vain, but he was surely right. He sported a neat, slightly over-sized moustache but no beard. You wouldn't call him handsome, perhaps, but with twenty-two, gentle, unstressed years under his belt he was certainly a presentable young man.

He was looking intently from the port side, busily making a sketch of the receding vista from which he planned to paint a scene when he got back home. As he scanned the scene, he caught sight of an elegant and rather lovely young lady leaning on the rail a little further on. She too was looking back intently, and a little wistfully, at the city and port of Hamburg they had just left. Frederick was not to be described as a "ladies' man" in any prejudicial way but he had a good eye and liked what he saw. He could not let this opportunity slip by; he strolled up to her, and rather shyly asked if she was a regular voyager on this line. As she spoke, it was immediately clear that she was German but Frederick, though born and bred in England, had an acceptable grasp of that language as his parents had been born and lived the first parts of their lives in Schleswig-Holstein where both German and Danish were commonly spoken. He introduced himself and leaned on the rail next to her.

Her name, he learned, was Else Monestein and she was going to join some old friends in Hull. Was she travelling alone or with a friend or relative? Alone. Frederick was impressed by her evident independence, especially in view of her obvious youth. For her part, she was looking closely at him as he talked and she discerned a class, a social standing, in him which pleased her. He spoke quietly but with some confidence despite his obvious limitations with her language. He dressed well and expensively, she thought, although she wondered about his limp bow tie. Nor was *he* disappointed after his first sighting; her voice was soft but bright, and he saw how carefully and tastefully she had dressed. She was most attentive and made no bones about her inspection of this stranger.

What about you; are you alone too? Yes; he'd spent the last three months in Schleswig-Holstein looking at where his family had come from. He explained that his parents had been born and bred in Kiel and that he had an uncle – Gerhardt *von* Baeber, would you believe – who had spent most of his life in Lubeck. He mentioned the title with some amusement really but Else's eyes widened at the sound of it. He asked her about her friends in Hull and learned that they were really friends of her parents who had left Bavaria about ten years ago in 1885. She went on to tell Frederick that her mother had died giving birth to a still-born, second daughter when Else was eight years old. Her mother had come from excellent stock, she said, and yes, she remembered mother very well, and indeed, had learned to cook from her. After mother's death, she had been raised by her father with help from his sister, Else's aunt, Gudrun. Father had owned a small delicatessen in Munich so that her experience and comprehension of food were reinforced. Father had died when Else was eighteen and left his few simple possessions and a small legacy to his only child, but held in trust by Gudrun until Else achieved her majority. When she had turned twenty-one, just a few months ago, she decided that she would leave Munich for good and seek her fortune in England, a country she had long read and wondered about. Where better to start than in Hull where she already knew someone. So she had her furniture and other possessions crated up and transported overland from Munich to Hamburg; they were with her right now in the ship's hold. Whereabouts in England did Frederick live? In Hull! What good fortune. Would she care for a drink? She was vaguely surprised when Frederick led her to the second-class saloon; but then she was travelling second herself.

They met several times during that short voyage and before they disembarked, exchanged addresses – Frederick's and that of Else's friends. They were remarkably smitten by each other after so short an acquaintance but then we know how that can happen, don't we? And so it was that, after just a couple of weeks back in Hull, Frederick called at the home of Herr und Frau Hauptmann in Westbourne Avenue, which by one of life's trivial coincidences, was situated less than a mile from Frederick's house in De Gray Street. Whether Else had expected or approved of it, the Hauptmanns assumed something of the role of protectors, *in loco parentis* as it were, so that their enquiring about Frederick's status and parentage was, perhaps, a little more forceful than he had expected. But he understood well enough, and without resentment, explained that his parents had both died a few years earlier – within a couple of years of one another – and that he had taken over the rent of their house in De Gray Street. Mother and father had left Schleswig-Holstein in their early thirties and had lived in Hull for the rest of their days. No he wasn't an only child but had an older brother, Louis, who was a professional photographer. Oh, Louis Baeber! We have seen his studio window in Spring Bank, the Hauptmanns exclaimed; he's very good. So there it was; respectability at the unseen hand of his brother! Frederick was welcomed and encouraged to take Else for a stroll round Pearson Park.

In somewhat less than six months, Fred proposed and Else accepted. Frederick had found a delightful and most attractive fiancée and Else saw a way to rejoin her mother's class, and presumably, wealth. It seemed that they were made for each other. They were married in August 1896 in front of a small gathering of friends – and Louis as the only relative – in Saint Charles Borromeo Roman Catholic Church in the centre of Hull. Else was given away by Herr Hauptmann, and Louis was best man. They spent a week in a hotel on South Cliff in Scarborough for their honeymoon. As soon as they returned to Hull, Else had her furniture removed from storage in a warehouse in the High Street (it had not been fashionable and "high" since Charles II's day) and transported to De Gray Street where she set forth to feminise the house and to create as elegant a residence as she could. Appearances mattered very much to Else – rather less to Frederick, except insofar as matters of æsthetics were concerned, but he was happy enough to accede to her wishes where he could. In no time, they invited the Hauptmanns round for a genteel luncheon to thank them for their kindness and hospitality during Else's first few months in Hull. They gradually made a few friends in De Gray Street to complement some of Frederick's chums from his bachelor life and they were all individually invited for a meal in due time. Else certainly was an excellent cook and Fred knew how to present a table so that their luncheons and dinners acquired a degree of formality and elegance. Else was in her element.

There was a problem, however. To her considerable consternation, Else discovered that Frederick was nowhere near as wealthy as she had thought. He had never deceived her on the matter but she had naturally assumed that a man so well dressed and with such good manners as her beloved Frederick must have matching means. But Frederick was merely a tailor; he made good clothes, as his own suits advertised, but his income was modest. Although he worked reasonable hours at his trade, his clientele was small and he was rather blasé about enlarging it, preferring to put time into his painting. He did sell some pictures but not enough to really count financially. So it became more difficult to provide the sort of entertainment that Else wanted. For her part, she tried valiantly to compensate by innovative cuisine; she would prepare some quite exquisite seafood soups whose most significant ingredients were fish heads which she bought from the "leftover" trays in the fish shop for almost nothing. These might be followed by well-disguised scrag-end of mutton or beef brisket, complemented with clever combinations of quite common vegetables. She was, indeed, a good and inventive cook. What went into her puddings and sweets was a mystery of mysteries, and more to the point, cheap. So the Baebers were able to maintain a fine face. Provided, that is, that they pulled their horns in for the rest of the week. They may not have been well heeled but they could make a show.

    Two years later, Else gave birth to a daughter, Babette. She was a somewhat quiet child but seemed quite clever and was always happy to play on her own. She did have friends of her age in the street but she tended to prefer her own company. She was five years old and beginning to read when company was thrust upon her in the form of a little brother, to be christened Arno George Frederick. He was a nice little fellow with fine, fair hair and a delicate-looking face, not too unlike his father's. Babette was unimpressed and took to her books. Three years later, a third child was born to Else and Frederick, a second daughter they named Honor Elspeth. They aspirated the aitch in Honor. And they stopped there; three children were enough and as many as they could hope to raise. The family was complete. The house in De Gray Street was never really quiet again. Honor and Arno got on together from the beginning; Honor loved to be naughty and Arno assumed a protective role. Parents were rather more formal and stern in those days, of course, but Frederick was a tolerant and easy-going father except when he was obliged to enforce mother's rules.

    As the years passed and Frederick did nothing to improve his financial position, Else's disappointment grew. In today's climate, their marriage might have been dissolved but then was then. Of course, the children were protected from all marital turbulence. One thing, however, continued to hold them together; they both loved to impress friends and neighbours, to play a part, to advertise a superior quality of life which, as far as Else was concerned was to be equated with wealth, while

Frederick saw it more as an expression of good taste. Christmas Eve 1911 was quite typical of the Baebers' exuberant style.

Snow had been falling in Hull for a couple of days and had lain quite heavily already. The fires in the lounge and dining room had been lit early that morning and were now established and burning quietly in their grates. The house in De Gray Street was more toasty than it had been since the previous Christmas. Far more of the wall lights had been lit than in the days immediately before and there were several shielded candles judiciously placed on side tables and the bureau. A Christmas tree in one corner reached almost to the high ceiling and had just been decorated with some of the loveliest baubles you could imagine. Not those plastic, coarse balls and little dolls of today but *bon-bons* made of the thinnest and lightest Lauscha glass you could imagine. They were Else's pride and joy, brought with her from Munich. Some were maybe eight inches long and others were so intricate that they had spaces within spaces, like Russian dolls, twinkling in delicately varied silvered shades as they reflected the gas and candle lights all around. They were, of course, extremely fragile. Only Frederick and Else themselves would dress the tree, for Arno and Honor were still far too young to be trusted. At eleven years old, however, Babette *was* old enough but wasn't interested in such silly things. She liked reading books and didn't indulge in the childish pranks of her younger siblings. Honor couldn't care less. She had red hair and was five years and four months old. Arno was eight and adored his little sister. He knew her hair wasn't bright red. She wasn't a carrot-top nor was she auburn but had a mix of red and fair hair; not really a strawberry blonde though, more of a reddish mouse. Someone had told her, however, that redheads were vivacious. She didn't quite know what "vivacious" meant but later, after she learned, she agreed. Heartily. Honor often laughed and smiled but far more with her eyes than with her mouth. She would purse her lips and lingeringly say, 'Oh!' or 'Aw!' perhaps, while her eyes opened wide and twinkled like the baubles on the tree. She could really put it on. She had already discovered many ways of being naughty in her short life. Fine crystal dishes of walnuts and Brazils, crystallised ginger and a box of dates were to be found artfully scattered around. Honor liked walnuts and crystallised ginger and would nick one or two but only while Arno was looking. 'Family, hold back,' he remonstrated, for there were only a very few dishes and they were only small and Mama had warned them repeatedly.

'Oh!' said Honor with her shining eyes. 'FHB, pooh!'

Uncle Louis and Aunty Gelda were coming for dinner that evening. The Baebers had also invited the Elvins and the Hauptmanns. Laura and George Elvin, "a most elegant couple", lived in Park Street which was to be found in "a most elegant residential area" of Hull. Frederick had met them on board ship on his outward trip to Schleswig-Holstein in that summer when he later met Else for the first time. The Hauptmanns were old friends – no, more acquaintances – of Else from Bavaria. They were the folk who looked after Else in her first six months in Hull, you remember. Her family were really well-to-do, Else informed anyone and everyone, and nobody could doubt it from her elegant dress and poise. She and Frederick made a handsome couple who were, without doubt, going to succeed – maybe not quite yet but in an assuredly near future. Few people in De Gray Street mixed with the likes of the Elvins or the Hauptmanns. Louis and Gelda could attest to that.

A goose had been prepared early that morning. It had been stuffed with Else's secret sage, apple and onion concoction; potatoes were ready for roasting; sprouts were trimmed and crossed; bread sauce was in mind. There would be a simple tomato soup to begin, and of course, Christmas pudding afterwards. The pudding had been made more than a year earlier and would be beautifully mature by now. The table had been polished to a gleaming perfection. It had been laid for hours. Each setting was graced with one of a huge set of the finest circular crochet doilies which were Else's pride and joy, and rightly so, for their delicacy was testament to the hours of work she had put into them. The cutlery was polished and shining and carefully placed in the correct fashion and precisely in line with the adjacent settings, so too the beer glasses. There were pepper and salt cellars at each end of the table. Candles surrounded with holly were placed in the middle, ready to be lit. Damask napkins on each side plate were topped with crackers; Fred had found some inexpensive ones in the market. Mistletoe had been hung in front of the square bay window. One bottle each of sweet sherry, port, whisky, gin and advocaat were prominently placed on the bureau surrounded by gleaming glassware; not crystal, unfortunately. The curtains were half-drawn – enough to make the rooms cosy but not too much to hide the splendour from anyone passing by outside. Everything had been checked repeatedly by Frederick and Else; everything was as perfect as it could be.

Earlier in the afternoon, presents wrapped in coloured tissue had been placed under the tree. There were two for each of the children from their parents and two from their siblings, and four each for Mama and Papa – from each other and from each of the children. There were a few other ones too, something for each of the guests. It all looked lovely. A warm, slightly alcoholic aroma permeated the house.

Gelda and Louis were the first to present themselves – by arrangement rather than by coincidence, of course. One wished to be properly attentive to the Hauptmanns and Elvins when they arrived so it was best to get all the family greetings over and done with beforehand. And everyone knew that Louis was altogether more amenable after a snifter or two and anyway, there wasn't enough whisky to go round everybody with safety. Gelda was happy with a small port and lemon and the children just had lemonade. Mama had another beer. Lots of hugs and kisses all round, although Babette was somewhat retiring from all that. Louis had brought his camera and tripod with him to record the happy occasion. Everyone agreed that Louis was an excellent photographer. And of course, everybody knew about Fred's painting; several of his Scottish Highland scenes of bracken, gorse and heather graced the walls of this house in De Gray Street. Honor offered the dish of Brazils. Else breathed an FHB. Father was telling Gelda of how he had met the Elvins, when the Hauptmanns arrived.

Neither Honor nor Arno remembered the Hauptmanns. This was only their second visit since Else and Frederick had married. It was inevitable that there would be much reminiscing about Bavaria and the "old times" and inevitably, the children were not interested, not even Babette really, who was deeply into her book. *We* might have found the Hauptmanns' accent a little daunting but not the children, for it was much the same as Mama's. One presumes that Fred liked the accent; after all, he had married it! It seemed that Bavarians were still arguing about whether they were really Germans or, as many die-hards would have it, that Bavaria would never be completely swallowed by Westphalia. All the while, Frau Hauptmann's eyes were dashing hither and thither around the room, missing nothing.

'I see you still have your mother's table, Else,' she said, indicating the renaissance revival, German oak table in the lounge. It was one of the pieces Else had brought with her when she moved to Hull some fifteen years earlier. Frederick was not especially taken with the Hauptmanns but he understood that Else wanted to impress them, to justify her decision to leave Bavaria for good and make a new life with him in England. He too was in the business of impressing visitors, not really because of impeachable and dishonourable reasons but more because he just liked to be admired. He could put on a show. He was a good tailor and he wore some of his own threads to advantage. Else was striking and dressed well. Neither let the other down.

When the Elvins arrived, all attention was refocussed onto them. They were unknown to everyone except Frederick so there were many introductions, recollections of a sea crossing and enquiries about Fred's relatives in Schleswig-Holstein. The old saw about the place being part of Denmark or of Germany, depending upon it being a Tuesday or a Thursday, raised the usual titters. Though Frederick had been born and raised in England, his continental affiliations were clear enough. His attraction to Else, however, had absolutely nothing to do with her being Bavarian; his keen eye for beauty had settled his fate quickly enough.

Anyway, Fred was explaining to one and all that a summer spent travelling in Schleswig-Holstein, exploring some diary entries of an uncle – he was a *von* Baeber Else interjected – in the hope of meeting some of his immediate antecedents, had been interesting up to a point but not as informative as he had wished. He had, in any case, enjoyed his time there and had developed an easy-going affection for the place.

Honor was tugging at Mama's sleeve. Was it time for the presents yet? Christmas Eve was the day, after all, for all those who followed the continental ways and, as the children would have to go to bed rather soon after dinner, the ceremony should take place before that – in Honor's view, now. The guests had already made their contributions to the pile of gifts under the tree so there was a lot to get through. 'Yes, alright, children, you may begin,' said Mama.

The ensuing frenzy was far more decorous than we might see today but it was a scene that would be recognised all over the world in any middle-class family. Frederick replenished drinks to keep the adults distracted, and perhaps a little more tolerant of the children's antics. All agreed that it was a charming sight and in truth, the evening was made as much by it as by the splendour designed by Mama and Papa. The presents within the family were beautifully wrapped but simple. The children's most lavish gifts came from the guests. Uncle Louis set up his tripod and insisted that everyone should form a group and keep absolutely still for what seemed an age. There followed so many thank yous and kisses that adult conversation could hardly recommence before everyone was summoned to the table.

The children sat together at one end, Babette in the middle, facing Papa at the other end, with Arno and Honor on either side. One would not presume to record every mouthful consumed at this feast; but feast it was, for, as we know, Else was an excellent cook (the family cry was, "Just look what Mama can do with a fish head"; it was true but sadly rather frequent). Beer, lemonade and water were on hand, a glass of brandy was flamed over the Christmas pudding, everyone had their fill and there was some goose left over for cold cuts the next day. Happiness reigned over the party, the visitors were duly impressed and Mama glowed with pride. Honor and Arno were bundled off to bed while Babette, though having the choice to stay up for a while or not, chose to retire to her bedroom with her book. The eight adults wandered into the lounge to enjoy the rest of the evening. Gelda had brought a box of fine chocolates which were passed around while Frederick poured some more drinks. They chatted about Carmichael's jewellery shop in town which had opened a few years earlier but was now expanding into fine china and crystal. Had they heard that the new cinema opened last December in Anlaby Road, and called the *Kinemacolour Palace*, was having problems with its colour films and it was rumoured that it might revert to just playing black and white pictures? Oh! These fancy colour films will never catch on, it was decided; but they had a good piano player in there. Where did Else get her lovely dress from? This conversation was getting a little dangerous. A boutique in Munich was mentioned. Mrs. Hauptmann hadn't heard of it. It was thought to have closed a couple of years ago or changed its name maybe. Else was very good with her hands. Ever tactful, Louis drew attention to Fred's oil paintings.

Upstairs, Honor and Arno should have been asleep but they were still showing off their presents. They knew that tomorrow there would be cold goose and more Christmas pudding so that was alright. And they wouldn't have to play FHB. Tomorrow, they would wear their everyday clothes and go out and throw snowballs and build a snowman. Only after church, though. Mama insisted on going to church on Christmas Day. Honor didn't think that Papa was keen. Mama came up and they had to climb into their beds at last. It had been a lovely day.

Across the Pennines

There were many changes during the next seven years, but without doubt the most dramatic had been Papa's leaving Mama to live on his own in Blackburn across the Pennines. It was not difficult to see why, as far as his brother Louis was concerned. Else had hopes far beyond Frederick's means and simply would not miss any opportunity to humiliate him in front of the children, his brother and sister-in-law, and anyone else, if it came to that. Frederick was a good tailor; he earned a fairly steady wage which seemed secure enough but there were no opportunities for advancement. Even if there had been, Frederick was content enough with what they had. Else repeatedly announced that she had married beneath her, but truth to tell, she had misunderstood Fred's nature from the beginning and resented his indifference to restoring to her a position she had never actually known. It was not an unusual story but it brought pain just the same. So, coincidentally just before the Great War came to an end, Frederick jumped ship. He found a little house to rent in Blackburn and set up a small tailoring business there, working from home. He sent postal orders back to Else every fortnight to keep her and the children going. After a while, and very quietly, Else began to make dresses for sale. She didn't work very quickly at it but she made rather superior garments which fetched a decent price. Arno and Honor had left school in their twelfth years and Arno had been earning money for the last two and a half years as a junior clerk in a solicitor's office near the Land of Green Ginger in the old part of central Hull. So the family was able to survive, overall, in pretty much the same financial circumstances as before Papa had left. Babette, who had changed her name to Jeanette – and, later, Jean – by this time, was nineteen years old and had her own job in a publisher's office.

Honor and Arno had no real idea why their parents had decided to live apart. Honor was only nine years old at the time and her brother was barely three years older. In 1916, marriage problems were far less discussed than now, and in any case, you didn't, did you? Their elder sister, Babette, though five years older than Arno, probably knew little more. Not that Honor and Arno would have gleaned anything from her. She was just too old for them. She led her own, bookish life in the publisher's office and was virtually invisible to her younger siblings as they rode their bicycles or went fishing together for tadpoles in the little stream they had found just out of the city of Hull, which lies on the Humber estuary in East Yorkshire. Honor and Arno were bosom buddies. As ever, Honor dominated and Arno was happy that she did.

It was in June 1919 that Arno proposed to his sister that they should take off for a long summer break to visit their father in Blackburn across the Pennines. Their plan was to base themselves with their father for a month and to hire or borrow a couple of bicycles on which they would explore as much of Lancashire as time would allow. Arno had visited his father for a week during the previous summer and had cycled all the way to Blackburn and back to Hull, crossing the hilly spine of northern England, but it was too far for his younger sister, even though she undoubtedly had the spirit. And, make no mistake, Honor had spirit. On that occasion, Arno had taken a week's leave from the solicitor's office where he worked as tea boy and general factotum. This time, he quit his job completely, in favour of the long summer adventure, confident that he would find another on his return. Honor was still at school so they had set their departure date for the first Thursday after the end of term. It had been nearly three years since the family had all lived together. Honor missed her father very much so this holiday assumed considerable importance for her. They would take the train. Their mother had given them money to buy the tickets to Blackburn and it was understood from correspondence with Papa that he would finance their return journey.

There had been family train journeys in the past, particularly to Scarborough which everyone saw as *the* seaside destination in Yorkshire It was certainly more refined than Bridlington, they thought, although they had been there as well a couple of times. Today, though, was something rather special. Not only were they to travel on their own, but this journey would be much longer than anything they had undertaken before; and there were to be train changes as well.

A bus from the end of their street took the children directly to

Paragon Station in Hull, dropping them off at the huge iron canopy outside that impressive terminal. Grasping their small, carefully packed suitcases, they walked through the short tunnel-like passage under the splendid hotel that was part of that grand station, into the huge concourse, built in the Italian style, and up to the immense, polished-timber booking office in the middle. Honor opened her purse and handed their money to Arno to buy their tickets. They gawped for a minute or two at the extensive ironwork so high above them before being checked through onto the platform from where they marvelled again at the splendour of the arches supporting the roof to the whole enclosure. Steam and smoke were everywhere and there was so much noise. There couldn't be a busier station anywhere else in the world, thought Honor – or noisier. They knew that Hull was England's third busiest port after London and Liverpool and that made everything seem so much more important. They found a couple of seats in third and wondered what it would be like in first. They didn't see anyone get into first, though, and they did keep a watch. It seemed an age before they heard the guard whistle and felt the train shudder and slowly begin to move off. Outside the station, the tracks curved quite markedly, so that the children were able to look back out of the right-hand-side window of their compartment and see all five arches of the terminal building receding behind them. They were off.

Sooner than they had imagined, they came to the villages of, first Hessle, and then North Ferriby where Arno had cycled at one time. It was fun for him, trying to pick out landmarks from a different viewpoint, and a moving one at that. They saw some painters refreshing North Ferriby Station as they whistled past. Their brush strokes appeared frozen in time by comparison with the speed of their passing. There were to be two train changes on their journey – the first in Selby after about forty minutes and the second in Todmorden where they should arrive some two and a half hours after leaving Hull. There would be a twenty minute wait there for their final connection, which meant, and which had been planned for weeks in advance, that they would just have time to buy tea and toasted teacakes in the station buffet. That would be so grown up they thought, and its anticipation was almost as good as watching everything rushing past the window. The only other passenger sharing their compartment had left it in Selby, so they had a compartment in the new train all to themselves and they gabbled excitedly about the scenery as they went along. It wasn't clear whether that passenger had completely left the train in Selby or had merely sought a new compartment for some peace and quiet.

Todmorden Station was a fairly important centre for the rail network in those days. On the one hand, it served as a junction within the Manchester and Leeds Railway and east to Selby and Hull; and on the other, it formed a link with the Caldervale Line serving the area northeast of Manchester. So the railways had put little Todmorden on the map. It was certainly on the map as far as Honor and Arno were concerned, for its teacakes were delicious. For the umpteenth time that day, they checked that all their luggage – one suitcase for Honor and one for Arno – was with them. Mama had warned them about that repeatedly. It was just after half an hour past midday when they boarded their third train for the last leg to Blackburn, and as that would take barely an hour, they opened the sandwiches prepared for them by their mother straightaway. About a quarter of an hour later, the train entered a tunnel and they had to scramble to shut the window because of the smoke. It had a funny smell; you didn't want too much of it but there was something quite fascinating about that smell that lingered in their memories for years. The train was nearly on time as they drew into Blackburn. Honor and Arno were excited as they looked forward to seeing their father again.

Following instructions which their father had sent, they found the bus that would take them close to the house which he had rented since coming to Blackburn. So, after a short walk, they arrived around a quarter past two. At last! Honor excitedly ran to her papa and hugged him tightly; Arno and Frederick shook hands. There were two small bedrooms in their father's house, in addition to his own, so that the children had one each.

After they had unpacked their things and joined Papa downstairs, Frederick asked Honor to put the kettle on. She scurried off to explore the kitchen, to make tea, find some biscuits and lay a tray; and when they all reassembled, Papa asked about their journey and tried to listen as they told him about everything they had seen and how exciting everything was. It almost seemed like old times. Five o'clock came round and father told Arno to lay the table while Honor put together a plate of ham and a salad bowl for tea. Fred told them where to find some beer and lemonade for everybody. Though not *quite* like old times, it was lovely to sit down with Papa again. After a while, Arno asked father whether he and Honor would be able to borrow bicycles from any friend or neighbour for explorations of the countryside around. Frederick thought it might be possible occasionally. 'But only at the weekends, of course,' he added. Arno was puzzled by this answer.

Out of the Blue

They had been in Blackburn for only a few hours on that Thursday when the blow fell.

'You don't imagine that I can support you while you are here,' their father was saying. 'You will have to pull your weight and contribute to the costs of the household. Honor, you must run the house, do the shopping and cook meals while you're here. Arno, you will have to take a job to bring in some money. In fact, I've found a solicitor in town who needs an office boy and I have arranged for you to start at nine o'clock on Monday morning. Your weekly pay will help cover the expense of your and Honor's keep.'

The children's mouths hung open for this was absolutely out of the blue. They had come for a holiday and to see the father who had walked out from the family home nearly three years ago. Honor dashed off to the kitchen with tears in her eyes. Arno cleared the table and took the dishes out to her. Honor clung to him with tears of utter incomprehension in her eyes. They couldn't find any words. Arno tried to make some sense of it all with his father but Frederick just told him, 'It's all arranged. That's how it will be.'

The children went out for a short walk so that they could talk, but really, they couldn't. They fell into a silence of hurt, regret and incomprehension. When they returned, they bade their father goodnight and went straight to their rooms and to sleep.

The following morning, their father gave Honor a short list of groceries she should buy at the local shop. He gave her a little money from a groceries jar on the mantelpiece and told her that she must show him the receipt when they returned and put the change back into the jar. 'There's seven and six in there to start with,' he said.

Arno went with Honor on this first occasion, because he was free to do so but also to show her where the shops were, for he remembered from his visit the previous year. Father checked the receipt carefully when they returned and spiked it before locking it in his bureau. Arno enquired again about being able to borrow bicycles and father told him to ask Mrs. Mabbs three doors along. So, after a spot of lunch, they went in search of this lady. She was a really bubbly soul and asked who they were and where had they come from and did they enjoy the journey and how long were they staying with their father… and yes! Indeed my dears, you can borrow a couple of bikes. They belonged to her own children who were grown up now and only used them when they occasionally visited her and Mr. Mabbs so Honor and Arno could hang on to them while they were in Blackburn. What marvellous luck! And how generous. Even more, for they then accepted her invitation to have a cuppa and cake. What a nice lady. They were in a good mood when they returned to their father's house. A degree of contentment persisted for the rest of that day, as Honor began to think about an evening meal while father suggested a game of draughts with Arno. In the evening, father went off to do some tailoring in the front room. Left to themselves, Honor took up some knitting she had brought and Arno began to read one of the Sexton Blake detective stories he had with him. So the children's second day was rather easier and more placid than their first. And tomorrow was Saturday so they could look forward to a day in the country.

After breakfast, Honor packed some sandwiches for Arno and herself to take on their day out while Arno altered the heights of the bicycle saddles. The cycle frame was a bit large for Honor but a small adjustment of the handlebars fixed that alright. They were lucky, for the weather was fine again. Mind you, it had been fine ever since they had left Hull and seemed set to stay that way. They planned to cycle to Ribchester on the Ribble. It was only six or seven miles away according to signposts, so they could be leisurely about their outing. Honor was happy but a bit wobbly being perched so high as they set off. They were soon out of Blackburn and into some gently rolling, verdant countryside. Arno had always loved the country scene, especially if it was lush and the hills were not too steep. When they came within sight of the river, they left the road and wheeled their bikes down a gently sloping meadow towards the water. There was a small island in the river at that point; if they'd had a small boat, it would have been fun to cross to it. They weren't prepared for a swim, not having brought towels with them, so they just meandered around for a while admiring the view before climbing back to the road. A little further on, the road offered a left turnleading to a stone bridge over the river for access to Ribchester itself, so they took that turning and after a couple of miles came to the village. It was a typical Lancashire village for that area, with neat stone houses everywhere and there was a pub called *The White Bull*. They chose a downwards sloping path which they reasoned would circle back to the river. It took them past St. Wilfred's Church, and did indeed lead to the river, where it joined another track running parallel to the bank. After a short ride, they had left the village again and found an inviting grassy bank to settle on for their lunch. They had the place all to themselves; they were warm and happy. It would be good to do this every day of their holiday. Arno had temporarily forgotten that he had to present himself at a solicitor's office on Monday morning.

On Sunday, the children stayed at home with their father. Arno helped with a bit of house cleaning while Honor worked in the kitchen. Father was cutting in the front room. Later on, Arno read some more of his Sexton Blake novel while Honor played *patience*. A quiet day. It was, after all, what they had imagined their holiday would be.

Up with the lark on Monday morning, Arno spruced up as best he could, bearing in mind that he had not packed his best clothes, and set off soon after breakfast for the solicitor's office. Father had given him clear directions and a small sketch map so it wasn't difficult to find the place; he arrived at a quarter to nine in good time for his interview. He was ushered into the office of a Mr. Featherstone who turned out to be a kindly man of fifty-odd, Arno supposed. He was softly spoken and he gently outlined Arno's duties; they were much the same as those he had fulfilled in his job in Hull, as he explained to Mr. Featherstone, who was duly pleased. His new boss explained that his wages, as a juvenile, would be paid directly to Arno's father as had been arranged some weeks ago. This was a surprise at first, until Arno remembered that a similar arrangement in Hull had been bypassed because his father was absent from home and Arno had been deemed to be the "head of the household". Mr. Featherstone showed Arno where he could hang a coat – though he hadn't brought one to Blackburn for a summer holiday – where the kettle and tea making equipment were kept, and where the broom and dusters could be found. He was shown a small desk where he would copy some incidental documents. Much later, he was entrusted with the copying of a more important item and Mr. Featherstone was impressed by Arno's ability to produce a fair copy; as time went by, he was entrusted with several more important copy jobs. All in all, Arno settled in well and was liked, but of course, the job was nine to five, five days a week.

So it began and so it continued. Arno wasn't worked to death in the office and Honor wasn't worked to death in father's home. Nevertheless, they *were* worked and had only a little fun time after the evening meal, and of course at weekends. Towards the end of their fourth week in Blackburn, the children began to pack their cases for the return journey. After a while, their father noticed the half-loaded suitcases and asked what they were doing. They reminded him that their plan had been to stay with him for four weeks and that they planned to catch a train back to Hull tomorrow. Please could he give them their train fares as was promised.

'No, no; you can forget that,' replied their father. 'You're not going back; you are staying here with me. Everything is going very well here.'

They were staggered and protested very strongly that father had agreed in a letter before they had embarked upon their journey that he would pay their return train fares. However, their father was adamant and became rather angry. 'You are staying,' was all they got out of him.

Honor went off in tears and Arno walked away slowly in a cold fury. The trouble was that the children had absolutely no money of their own and so no means of getting away. They just couldn't believe that their father would, in effect, kidnap them like that.

A Plan

The weekend was coming up, so Honor and Arno determined to go off cycling again in the country, as they had every weekend they had been in Lancashire. They also decided to write a letter to their mother explaining the situation and asking her to send them a postal order immediately for their return train tickets; they posted it as soon as they left father's house on their Saturday ride. Otherwise, life continued as it had for the past four weeks while they waited for their mother to reply. Two weeks went by without their hearing from Mama. When would that postal order come? They were becoming increasingly worried.

Eventually, Honor came up with a plan which she and Arno discussed in her bedroom away from their father. She was in charge of the housekeeping money and proposed taking a little out of the jar every day until they had amassed enough for their tickets. Arno was doubtful. He pointed out that it wouldn't work because father insisted on receipts for everything Honor bought and the old man checked the money jar after each visit to the shop. But Honor had a plan. She would keep the accounts properly but use a little less of each grocery item every day so that she could accumulate a small stockpile and pocket the money next time she had to buy more. 'But what about the receipts?' Arno protested.

That had them stumped for a while until Arno had the idea of copying receipts from previous purchases; he was, after all, rather adept at making copies, as Mr. Featherstone could attest. So, between them, by theft and forgery, they would gradually accumulate enough cash for their journey back to Hull. It seemed a good plan, and every day, Honor secreted a little sugar, a potato or two, or whatever else, in the back of the pantry and pocketed a few pence each time she went to buy more groceries. Arno forged away and their subterfuge progressed very well. They were very careful about what they were doing and made sure that father was satisfied with Honor's housekeeping. Meanwhile, they continued to check the post every day but nothing came.

It took nearly five weeks for them to accumulate enough money for their tickets. What a magnificent effort! It was on a Monday that they packed their cases once more but this time they were extremely careful not to let father see what they were doing. Straight after breakfast the next morning, they very quietly brought their suitcases downstairs while father was in the front room attending to his tailoring. They left a brief note on the dining table and carefully crept to the front door.

Knew it All Along

Just before they got there, their father came out into the hallway and stopped them in their tracks.

'Just where do you think you're going?' he asked. Without waiting for an answer from the dumbstruck children, he continued. 'I told you that you were staying here. Did you really think that I didn't know about your filching money from the housekeeping? That's stealing. Hand it over. Now.' He took Honor's purse and emptied their carefully hoarded money out of it into his large cold hand and put it in his own pocket.

There was a short silence. And then, Honor screamed. She screamed very loudly; she screamed again, and again. She continued screaming at the top of her voice, with all her strength. Frederick became concerned lest his neighbours should hear. His was a row house so it was quite possible someone might think some violence was occurring. He tried to shush Honor up but she was having none of it. Arno didn't know what to do; he daren't hit his father and in any case, he wasn't strong enough to wrest the money back off him. Honor was rapidly becoming hysterical and her father was beginning to get really frightened. He tried to mollify her and promised to buy her a nice dress. She began to calm down, not in response to Frederick's coaxing but simply from exhaustion. She then did something which in retrospect she just couldn't believe she did. She spat in his face. She spat in her father's face, then ran up to her bedroom and barricaded her door with a chair. Her father didn't try to follow her, however, and told Arno to take their cases back upstairs and to calm her down. Later, Arno went up to see his sister and to comfort her as best he could. They just clung to each other in an effort to assuage a betrayal they just couldn't believe or comprehend.

After a while, Arno decided to go into the office. He had to apologise for his considerable lateness; he had planned to write a letter to Mr. Featherstone after he and Honor had returned to Hull. Anyway, he made some lame excuse and got on with his work but he was listless all day.

Indeed, he was listless for every day of that week and when the kindly Mr. Featherstone saw no improvement by the following Monday, he called Arno into his office and asked him what was wrong. After a while, Arno blurted out the full story of how their father had virtually kidnapped them and how he had caught them in their well-planned escape. The solicitor was appalled and angry to hear this story, and later that day while Arno was still in the office, went round to confront Frederick face-to-face. He informed him that it was shameful to treat anyone like that, let alone his own children; moreover, that it was illegal and that if necessary, he would initiate proceedings on the children's behalf. Of course, that last bit was a lie for their father had every legal right to demand their allegiance. Featherstone told Frederick to give them their fares and let them go back to their mother immediately. Fred was flabbergasted and angry, but scared and did as he was told. The children repacked their cases, had time to return their borrowed bicycles to Mrs. Mabbs, and then left immediately for the station and home. Thank you, thank you, Mr. Featherstone. Their nightmare was over.

The journey home seemed to pass quickly though they had time to have some tea and scones in Selby. Mr. Featherstone had given Arno a couple of pounds in gratitude for his good work, and 'in case your father doesn't pay up' so they were able to indulge themselves in the station buffet. As the train went through North Ferriby during the last few minutes of their journey, they saw that the painters had progressed to the far end of the station and had very nearly finished refreshing the fencing along the platform. The children had been away more than twelve weeks.

When they got home, they found Mama waiting for them. Mr. Featherstone had sent a telegram briefly explaining the circumstances and warning her of their imminent arrival. They were emotionally exhausted but so pleased to get home and Mama gave them hugs and a warm welcome. As they were eating their tea that evening, Arno asked Mama why she hadn't replied to their letter asking for their fares home. They learned that she had, in fact, sent them a postal order by return post. Clearly, father had intercepted it and said nothing. There was no way that they could ever forgive him for what he had done. Many years later, Arno did – somewhat reluctantly – offer his by then destitute father, temporary accommodation. Honor never forgave her father and never spoke to him again. That terrible shared experience established a very strong bond between Honor and Arno which was to be reinforced and to last all their lives and have repercussions on others.

Nobody died, there was no murder; this was just a simple tale of quite ordinary people, but ordinary people can feel extraordinarily strongly about events in their lives. One should never imagine that others' hurts simply vaporise in the warmth of a spring. Sixty-five years or so later, as an old lady, Honor told the story to her nephew, Mathew, and his wife with such vigour, clarity and hurt that one could see her reliving every moment as she did so.

PART 2
BILL and LEAH

Getting Settled

Two years later, Jean found a boyfriend and she wanted to marry him. The family never got to know his first name. He preferred Bowdie, short for Bowden, his surname. He was Canadian and a selfish bore in Honor's and Arno's opinions. They were probably right. He wanted to take Jean and get married in Toronto and so off they went. Jean was twenty-one years old and she made her home in Toronto for the rest of her life although she did return to England for a few visits over the years. Nobody else in the family seemed particularly concerned with her life choices. For years, she had been somewhat aloof although when Arno's son met her some fifty years later, he found her to be a somewhat diffident old lady; but age plays its tricks.

Else and Frederick continued their separate lives though they remained married, and Honor and Arno grew up steadily. By the age of nineteen, Honor had become rather striking. Her mother had been quite beautiful at that age and her father, though hardly film-star handsome, had certainly been presentable. Honor did not fit any classic form of beauty but her strong features, her sense of fun and her unfailing desire to shock made her appealing to men and women alike. She was just great fun. Arno, who had been a rather pretty boy as a small child, had grown a pencil-thin moustache in his late teens, wore his fine, straight hair parted exactly in the middle and combed back to give the overall appearance of a neat – almost elegant – smart young man. Arno was twenty-two when Honor fell head over heels in love with a bloke some nine or ten years her senior. He had a sporty open-top car and she loved being driven at speed in it and letting her hair get tousled in the slipstream. Her beau had probably already persuaded her into bed by the time Arno decided to make some enquiries and to follow him after he dropped Honor off one evening. Arno had a car of his own by this time. It wasn't in the same league as that of the boyfriend but it was still pretty desirable. It didn't take too much effort to find that lover-boy was married. Arno told Honor immediately and she broke off her relationship on the spot. Honor was no prude but she wouldn't stand for a liar and a cheat; actually, more to the point, she wouldn't tolerate being deceived herself. Once more, of course, her dear brother had come to the rescue in her life and their bond was duly further strengthened.

It was about this time that Arno signed up for a steward's job in the merchant navy. His ship sailed the Baltic and between Danzig – as Gdansk was then known – and Hull. He had always got on well with people. He was polite and courteous and could easily hold a simple conversation with strangers; he knew how to lay a table and to keep drinks glasses clean and polished so he fitted the job very well and he enjoyed it for a while. He quit when he was twenty-five years old, however, preferring then to take a job as a car salesman for Thompson's, a prominent car salesroom in Hull. Family members have frequently expressed amazement at his success in this job, which he held until World War II broke out in 1939 when Thompson's had to retrench and let half its staff go. One could not imagine anyone less likely to be a car salesman, but he enjoyed the job and was very successful at it. There was no way that Arno could bluff a potential buyer. He spoke the truth at all times and religiously described a car's attractions *and* its faults, but his charm and patent honesty won him many customers, and in the '20s and early '30s at least, he earned a very good wage. He really enjoyed the job, which certainly marked a high point in his earning capacity and job satisfaction. It was reasonable to describe him as a "good catch".

On many an evening, one could find Arno enjoying a drink in one of several watering holes around Hull, Cottingham and other villages nearby, and even as far afield as Beverley. He liked his drink – often a rum – and would spend a fair time in his favourite haunts, but he rarely got particularly drunk – or maybe one should say, perceptibly so. Some people are lousy drunks; others can hold it and themselves properly. Arno was a good drunk. He would say lots of silly things after a few too many but was never offensive or loud; after what he called "a bibful", he would go home, climb the stairs, undress and carefully fold and put away his clothes (even rolling up his socks into little balls before placing them in the top drawer of his tallboy), climb neatly into bed and fall sound asleep. A real gent. He would drive up to these pubs in one or other car he had on loan from Thompson's; and remember there was little, if any, censure in those days against drinking and driving. Presumably, major accidents were sufficiently uncommon because of the relatively empty roads that the law didn't get involved; indeed, it was not uncommon to see an off-duty policeman unsteadily leave a pub and drive off in his car.

It was on one of these evenings that Arno met an attractive, short, dark-haired girl who laughed a lot, liked a drink herself – as did the girlfriend she was with – and who was fun and real. They met several times like that and eventually, Arno asked her on a date to go to the "flicks" and a meal out. And so, and so… Her name was Leah Harris. She was Jewish and came from a large family. While proud of the Jewish race, she had little time for formal religion so that no problems arose with Arno, who though formally Catholic, cared nothing for his or anyone else's religion. He remembered times in his childhood when nuns would call at the family home in De Gray Street with, as he put it, a "begging bowl". The Baebers lived reasonably well as far as outside appearances were concerned, but as we well know, were actually close to the bread line. Arno told Leah about the Christmases they had enjoyed where his mother and father would show off to impress neighbours and acquaintances but would literally eke out food for most of the rest of the year. He resented those nuns regularly coming to the house and pressurising his mother to part with her last sixpence of the day – or even week – when her family were in such need themselves; they left a lasting impression. Anyway, with those negative memories, it was hardly surprising that Arno had little time for religion so that, as far as he was concerned, Leah's religious heritage meant equally little, provided, as he would say, it "wasn't pushed down your throat". Now, it seemed, Arno was well-off. The times had changed. To some extent, however, Leah was making a similar mistake to that of Arno's mother in that she had misunderstood the financial stability of her catch. Unlike Else, however, she had been brought up in England and spoke English with an English accent so that any misunderstanding was not to be laid at the door of language. Leah's and Arno's romance was founded on far shallower matters; they enjoyed each other's company and laughed at many of the same things. They were hysterical about the slapstick comedy in the silent movies of the day, especially the Keystone Cops and, of course,

Charlie Chaplin and Buster Keaton.

Leah's family had come to England from Latvia as did many Jews around the beginning of the twentieth century. Her parents were Isaac and Minna Hirschowitz; Minna's family name was Rosenfeld. Hirschowitz was a fairly common name, particularly in the Baltic States, and like most others with this name, Isaac anglicised it to Harris on taking up residence in England. As was Frederick, Isaac was a tailor, a skill he passed on to at least two of his sons. Isaac and Minna had eight children altogether. Louis was the eldest with Leah coming second, and as such, the eldest daughter. These two children and a third, Anne, were born either in Latvia or at sea on their way to England. Such is the story told in later years but they couldn't all have been born at sea; it seems that their official papers were either lost or concealed so that the exact birth dates and such matters were mislaid, invented or made official from word of mouth later. Biographers might have a merry time with all that, but within the family and their descendants, one doubts that it mattered much. The five further children were born in Hull where Isaac and Minna put down roots.

As the eldest daughter, Leah was expected to help her mother raise the rest of the family. The responsibilities of this *de facto* motherhood – especially when Minna was giving birth again – had robbed Leah somewhat of her childhood. She felt no strong resentment at this; it was simply a fact but one which inevitably came to mould her character and makeup. Minna died in 1921 when Leah was eighteen so her "mothering" days had continued for a few years more. She was effectively off the leash by the time she was twenty-five and met Arno. It is hardly surprising to find that she was intent on enjoying some freedom and a good time. Arno didn't really care much for most of Leah's siblings, largely because of their perceived Jewish clannishness. An exception was Anne, who was, like Leah, much more open-minded, especially with respect to gentiles. That Anne was rather more physically attractive than Leah's other sisters probably influenced Arno's opinion too. Leah became acquainted with Honor, of course, and the two got on together passably well, due in no small measure to Honor's vivacious nature. Even so, it was Honor who first called Leah Leo. It sounded right somehow: Leo and Arno. The fact that Leo is a man's name didn't stop

Honor any less than her insistence on aspirating her own name. Leah's son later wondered whether this aspiration was another manifestation of the Catholic insistence on aspirating the eighth letter of the alphabet whenever they could. It seemed, he would observe, that they were quite blind to the spelling of the eighth letter as aitch. Anyway, Leah became Leo for the rest of her life, except of course within the Harris family and her own head.

Leo and Arno became closer over the next eight years, enjoying life together, often driving to Scarborough to see the Italian Gardens on the South Cliff. They would stroll, arm-in-arm, both "dolled up to the nines", as Arno would say, and, indeed, they *were* both elegantly dressed. Arno was fastidious in his choice of well-tailored sports jacket with fine twill trousers, his tie knot formed perfectly with a dimple in the middle, a handkerchief in his breast pocket, his shoes beautifully shined – or brushed when he wore suedes. In those early days, Leo had some rather fine dresses which were complemented with beautiful shoes and handbags. They would follow the paths of these exquisite gardens in Scarborough which Arno had known and loved for years and on down to the oval, open-air public swimming pool built onto the rocks of that rough beach, take a seat in the café there and enjoy a pot of tea and some cakes while listening to a small brass band playing popular favourites. Afterwards, they would amble northwards, admiring the view of the castle on the headland separating the north and – socially, far more desirable – south bays, until they reached the funicular rail lift. Walking *down* through the Italian Gardens was one thing; climbing *up* them was quite a different matter; the funicular was a godsend. Actually, they did make the climb on occasion but would get quite puffed in the process. On other days, they drove to Bridlington and walked around the harbour to view the fishing boats forever coming and going and unloading their catch. A favourite winter pastime was to see the Boxing Day Meet on the outskirts of Beverley. Neither knew anything about horses or fox hunting; they simply liked the sight of the horses and hounds, of the posh ladies and gentlemen in their pink, astride the horses and taking a sip or two of punch before they moved off for the hunt proper. After watching the colourful spectacle for half an hour or so, Arno would drive them back into town to the Beverley Arms Hotel where they could ape the local toffs and take a drink or two at the bar before going back to Hull to enjoy a Boxing Day cold plate. They looked the part but couldn't altogether afford it. It wasn't really social climbing; they didn't know how to do that and, in later years at any rate, they certainly didn't have the wherewithal. In any case, they enjoyed laughing – often sneakily – at the pretensions of others – surely a lesser sin.

While Arno's and Leo's romance blossomed, Honor had not been quiet. She had met a new young lad who had the priceless virtue of not already being married. Bill Denton was a most solid citizen. Arno, Honor and Leah had all left school around twelve years of age as was very common in those days. For girls, it was commonly thought, that didn't matter for they would be supported in due course by their future husbands. Arno's lack of any further education meant that his horizons were limited, and as the years rolled by, it became more and more obvious that his financial possibilities were strongly curtailed also. Bill had come from a very poor family of farm labourers in East Yorkshire. He had enjoyed none of the visual or near-eclectic benefits which Arno and Honor had sensed from their semi-continental upbringing, or which Leah had partially gleaned from being a member of a large Jewish family. However, Bill had rather more brains than his mother or father and even his elder brother. That brother had left the hardship of the land and gone to sea – or, to be more exact, had found a job as a lighterman. He had escaped the grinding hardship of his youth and he set to persuading Bill to do the same. Bill was indeed impressed but he took another route, for because he was clever enough, he successfully enrolled as a student in the Trinity House naval school in Hull. There he learned a fair modicum of mathematics, especially trigonometry, geography and even some French. In due course, he passed his mariner's exams and got his ticket to sail the seas. Bill had pulled himself up by his own determination and hard work, and in time, he got his reward.

He had been at sea for a relatively short time when he first met Honor. He had a twinkle in his eye and those eyes were utterly transparent; he adored Honor and they told the world. Honor wrapped Bill round her little finger. She made no secret of doing it and Bill made no complaint. Bill was solidly built and very strong. Normally, he was so quiet and gentle that you would never suspect his physical strength, but years later, his son told how of how Father had picked up a heavy wheelbarrow filled with clay – picked up, not pushed – and hurled it some ten feet from him. He had stubbed his toe, you see. Anyway, big, gentle, pipe-smoking Bill was in the merchant navy and had sailed to just about everywhere on the globe. When Honor first clapped eyes on him, he was studying for his exams as a navigator, using trigonometry and tables to compute courses manually, rather more basic – and, of course, far harder – than pushing buttons on a computer as is done today. Some years later, after he had passed his navigator's and master's diplomas, he got a job as pilot on large ships navigating some of the more treacherous sea passages around the world. The trouble was that this kept him from his beloved for rather too long at a time, so as the years went by, Bill focussed on being a North Sea pilot. It was the same sort of job of course, and quite complex at times as harbour entrances around the North Sea can be difficult, but it meant that his absences from Hull and Honor were shorter. Honor and Bill often met up with Leo and Arno for an outing in Yorkshire, a meal out and a drink or two. If Bill was at sea, Honor might join Arno and Leo by herself. Bill and Leo got on well, although a pattern began to emerge of the strongest relationship on show being the brother-sister bond. Nothing shameful, of course, simply the strength of years of shared experience and trouble. In the beginning, Bill and Leo were not at all worried for they both believed that the bonds of love and matrimony should trump those of sibling loyalty.

Well, matrimony did come to Honor and Bill relatively soon after he became a full-time North Sea pilot. They were married in 1930 when Honor was twenty-four years old and Bill twenty-seven. Bill's job was well rewarded and they set about looking for a home together, fairly quickly finding a modern semi-detached house on Swanland Hill in North Ferriby, about eight miles from the centre of Hull. The decision to move out of Hull into a village was prompted mostly by Honor's love of the country even though she had never actually experienced living outside a city. It turned out to be a good decision. They were very happy there, made a lot of friends, particularly Honor – Bill being away so much, of course – and enjoyed the views of open farmland and of the wide Humber Estuary from their front windows. Bill took a large mortgage on the house, which cost eight hundred pounds but he could manage that well on his pilot's salary. He left most home matters to Honor, not only because of his long absences piloting, but because the far stronger-minded Honor had home-building flair and an artistic sense inherited from her father. On the other hand, all money matters were kept in Bill's hands, not so much because he was the breadwinner, but simply because Honor was neither interested in such affairs nor particularly competent. Solid Bill was a safe man all his life, so Honor's life acquired a stability she had never known before. Bill did a little gardening out back where they had planted fruit bushes and vegetables in contrast to the floral displays in the front. Mind you, gardening was something new for both of them. There had been little land in De Gray Street and Bill's family background had been too poor and disadvantaged to have the time or money to play with things like that. Indeed, Bill's career was a testament to his determination and nous; he really had got out from under. Maybe Honor hadn't quite replaced the tempestuous love affair of her youth but she had found contentment and a safe, quiet and financially rather comfortable life. Her happiness was marred slightly, however.

Bill bought a piano, an upright Bechstein, which was a lovely instrument. He had learned to play with a fair degree of make-believe over the years; he had a pleasant touch but hit rather too many wrong notes; unruffled, he would fluff over these without breaking the rhythm. He played the classics mostly and used to refer to Mozart's *Rondo alla Turca* as Mozart's Turkey Trot. Many a spouse would have been pleased to have a pianist in the home, but Honor's well-developed artistic bent failed utterly to stretch to music. She was completely tone-deaf and heard all music as annoying noise. When Bill played, she absented herself and went off to read a romance paperback or do barbola work.

Bill bought Honor a couple of first-class fur coats and one or two fine pieces of jewellery. She loved these markers of wealth but mostly for their own sake.

'Feel that!' she would say, stroking the sable. 'Look at that colour!' she urged as she let her emerald and diamond ring twinkle in the sunshine. She and Arno had both inherited their father's eye. Yes, she loved her baubles for their æsthetic merits; but she also loved being able to show them off. She was never nasty about this; she was only human.

Bill would look on adoringly and grin. He even seemed to smile when Honor gave away so much of his hard-earned money to all and sundry, and that despite Bill's own history of coming from a cash-strapped background. Honor was known by everyone for her generosity. In part, she did it in order to show that she could, but mostly she did it because she wanted to help people in need. Everybody loved Honor. Don't make the mistake of thinking that she was loved because of what she gave. She was loved because of her personality, her vivacity. She liked being outrageous. She was fun to be with. Bill went unnoticed but he didn't care one jot. A central motif in Honor's and Arno's lives was their sense of something not far removed from superiority. It wasn't that they looked down on others, rather that they enjoyed a feeling of isolation and protection from the less agreeable things in life. That had been inculcated in them by their parents – parents, mind you, who were close to being as poor as church mice!

Honor and Bill completely shared one thing, though. Tony was born in April, 1936. Bill was as proud as punch to be a father and Honor took to motherhood extremely well, at least insofar that she would cuddle and touch their son endlessly. His parents spoiled him rotten. He looked like his father but took after his mother. A pity, really, for Honor, though gay, was frivolous but with Bill's rock-solid stability behind her, all was well. Tony, on the other hand, had to make his own way in the world. Although Tony took after his mother, he missed out on Fred's skills in the visual arts. Instead he inherited, and indeed bettered, his father's linguistic skills. He played the piano, like his dad. Exactly like his dad. Just kept on going through all the bum notes and didn't stop. But Tony's number one quality was his personality. He became, even as a young lad, an accomplished raconteur and mimic. He was such fun to be with. The genes were with him.

Now in those days of the Eleven Plus exams, there came a fraught time for parents and children alike. I'm not so sure it's any different nowadays even though the structures have altered. It was, however, a crossing-point when the rest of a child's life seemed to be determined. Honor and Bill naturally wanted the best for Tony. Tony was undoubtedly gifted, with his taste for foreign languages, his not insignificant piano-playing ability, his truly excellent memory for speeches in plays and of course his undoubted interpersonal skills. But these were not qualities that were examined in the Eleven Plus examinations. Tony achieved little. His parents were, quite naturally, upset for they had wanted him to attend the best school which Hull could offer, a minor public school called Hymers College, which admitted both scholarship and fee-paying pupils. In light of Tony's poor Eleven Plus results, they decided to buy his education. Bill could afford to do it, so why shouldn't they do so?

Meanwhile, Leah's and Arno's marriage was a long time coming but it did come and it lasted, although it was sorely tried later on by Arno's financial downturn. That began as World War II broke out. The bottom of the market fell out of the motor trade and Arno, along with many of his mates, lost his job. Leah, ever cautious, had previously opened her own bank account and saved some of her housekeeping money over the years. When she and Arno decided to buy their own house, she was in a position to obtain a mortgage on a semi-detached house in a pleasant and leafy part of Hull. The mortgage had to be taken out in Leah's name, of course, because of Arno's temporary unemployment at that time and it was possible because she had her own bank account, something which was not too common for middle class wives at that time. Arno tried many jobs during and after the war but never again saw anything like the financial comfort of his younger life.

In due course, Leah gave birth to their only child, a son they named Mathew. He was born three years after Tony. Mathew was the spitting image of his dad but he took after both his parents in other ways as you'd expect. Arno, like Honor, had demonstrated a fair facility with pen and pencil but neither seemed to have a strongly-developed creative imagination. Fred had had that. Mathew had it too, but to be fair, his creativity was mental rather than physical. He was dextrous enough but only in the way of someone who could cut paint into a window frame well. Mathew's strength lay in his imagination and intelligence. He always believed that much of that had come from his mother's side of the family. Later, he came to see that there were contributions from both sides but in quite different ways. Anyway, he was a clever boy and did well at school with ease in those subjects which interested him, which were science and maths. He was a happy kid even though he had only a few, albeit close, friends. He was as introverted as Tony was extroverted. He always admired his cousin but well knew his own strengths, so was in no way overawed by Tony's *bonhomie*. In his mid-teens, when our tale matures, Mathew spent much more time with his mother than with his father and had begun to understand them both as people as well as parents. You wouldn't call him a mummy's boy though, if only because of Leah's undemonstrative style – again, so different from Honor's. There was no "touchy-feely" business in that household, something which Leah felt guilty about but which did not bother Mathew at all. He gradually developed a great love and admiration for his mother, of which his dad was tolerantly aware.

The couples had kept in close touch if only by virtue of the strong brother-sister bond enjoyed by Arno and Honor begun in their earliest years and tested in the fire of their experience in Blackburn. They had gone their separate ways insofar as they had each found partners and begun to raise children, but none of that weakened their bond one jot. Friends almost certainly didn't notice anything but both Leah and Bill did, and at times, it irked them. It likely irked Leah more than Bill simply because Bill was so often away from home, guiding a ship into some harbour or other. Leah, on the other hand was reminded about the special relationship quite often. From the earliest days of Arno's and Leah's relationship, Honor had stamped her mark. You remember that she hadn't liked the very old Yiddish name Leah, and quite possibly was less than keen for a match between her brother and a Jewess. She had persuaded Arno to call his girlfriend Leo, despite that being a man's name. Leah had accepted it, though with some misgivings. Later, after she and Arno married, she copped it from her own relatives for "marrying out". Truth to tell, this particular piece of nasty stupidity emanated from just one of her siblings, a sister who turned out to be a nauseatingly religious bigot. Leah's sister, Anne, also married out but suffered far less abuse. For the most part, however, irritants caused by the strong brother-sister bond were minor but oft repeated. Arno would dash off to Ferriby to paint a room for Honor, for example, even when there were jobs for him to do at home. Or there might be other trivial, though time-consuming, errands. At one period around the time of our main story, Arno was trying to earn a little extra money by making tea trays which he decorated with coloured paper flowers held under glass. Each tray took a fair time to construct and he made little money from the enterprise. Nevertheless, he would take time off to make a magazine rack for Honor. He did it in recognition of the odd couple of quid she would slip him on one of his errands for her. That was a nice thing for him to do but it amounted to a sort of double payment, really. Leah saw all this, occasionally complaining but mostly keeping silent. The trouble with repeatedly keeping silent, of course, is that the accumulated hurt builds. While all this should not be exaggerated overly, Leah felt that she, Arno's wife, came off second best to Honor, Arno's sister. Bill was silent about all these things but he had a wily intelligence and he saw it all and sympathised with Leah. She saw that he did and was grateful.

The Poor Relations

It was around 1953 when Arno walked out of his job as a weekly fee collector for a company which supplied wired radio around Hull. It was a lousy and demeaning job but all he had been able to find at the time. He broke down in tears when he told Leah and Mathew what he had done. Mathew never forgot that scene. His sympathy for his dad was immense but he resolved never to be in such a position himself. Trouble was, there was no money coming into the house at all. Leah had always been a careful housekeeper and saver so that there was a little in her bank account, but really only enough to carry them for a very few weeks. But then, out of the blue, Arno found another job. He was to be a travelling salesman for a local hardware factor and brush manufacturer. He was to sell to general stores around much of Yorkshire. The pay wasn't marvellous but it was quite a bit better than he got from his last three jobs. The greatest boon of all was that he was supplied with a car. He'd always had a car when he was a car salesman but never since. He was ecstatic! Not only that, he was given considerable leeway in how he organised his routes and hours. He did well in his new job and earned small bonuses. He kept that job till he retired many years later. So it seemed that Arno's household had found some financial security at last. It's true to say that a modicum of happiness reigned over the place.

In due course, Mathew's turn for these Eleven Plus examinations came around. He not only passed but did so sufficiently well to gain a scholarship at Hymers. This surprised everyone and was a great source of pride to both Mathew and his mother. Arno took the news in a quieter tone because he saw that it would put Honor's nose somewhat out of joint. Mathew, however, saw none of that but Leah did and kept very quiet. She began to feel some equalisation between the Baebers and the Dentons.

The two families met up regularly, most often but not exclusively in the Denton's place in Ferriby. The Baebers would drive there for Sunday tea, which almost invariably meant cold ham or tongue with a salad, followed by a trifle covered with thick, artificial cream. That cream was, of course, a hangover from the days of rationing in the war. Many people had become acquainted with the stuff during those days, got to like it, and then found the real stuff a little too sour. Up till 1953, Mathew would play with Tony's clockwork railway set while the adults played cards. When Arno and family were hosts, the meals were pretty similar, though without the expensive tongue, and Mathew played with his Meccano set. Quite often, Tony wouldn't come, for his few years' seniority meant that he had found friends, and girlfriends of course, with whom to hang out. Mathew was as happy as Larry sitting on the floor, as often as not, under the card table with thick tobacco smoke all around while his mum and dad, aunt and uncle gambled at Newmarket for small change. Some years later, a new craze hit town and everybody played Canasta. By that time, Mathew had given up toys and joined in the fun.

Let's play a drum-roll now, good people, for it was in 1955 that Honor and Bill proudly displayed to Arno and family their new purchase. A television set. TV had been around in England for some years but was only just beginning to reach people on more modest incomes. Even so, not many people could afford a set. Certainly not Leah and Arno. There was a lot of snobbery around in those days to do with the possession of a TV set. One cartoon of the time showed a street with the chimney stacks of many houses bearing the typical H mast aerial but across the aerial for just one house was attached a sign with the message: "We have a washing machine!" Honor and Bill were, as ever, generous in sharing their new acquisition with their friends and family. They didn't do so in any snobbish way so far as anyone could see. They were, quite simply, happy to share. Arno never showed any sign of jealousy but then he always had a strong sense of what was proper; and in any case, he was happy for his sister. Leah certainly envied the in-laws' good fortune but she too always kept, let us say, a proper face. Mathew had been used to his parents' relative poverty for years and took it all for granted. Even so, from that time, it became the norm for Mathew and his parents to spend their Sunday afternoons with Honor and Bill. Sitting down to watch TV was quite an experience. Their set was decidedly an up-market model, something which only dawned on Mathew much later as he began to look at sets in shop windows. Their set was in the form of a free-standing, quite splendid, walnut-veneered cabinet boasting a pair of curved doors in front. Enclosed within, hidden from the discerning view, lay the unæsthetic, but rather essential, technical goodies. After tea, and after the washing up, everyone took a seat in front of those shiny cabinet doors waiting for Bill to open up and reveal the marvels within. They always watched the *Black and White Minstrel Show*. Arno and Honor, in particular, liked this musical extravaganza. There was no embarrassment in those days about the corking up for the black faces; it was a far more tolerant time. They simply enjoyed the melodies and the singing. Later on, they all tuned into their first cops-and-robbers show: *No Hiding Place*. It wouldn't pass muster today for a second but those were innocent days. Mathew asked his mum whether they would ever be able to afford a TV set but Leah explained yet again that they had far less money than Honor and Bill.

A Sense of Shame

One day, Leah asked Mathew for some advice. In truth she was simply using her son as a sounding board. She had decided to get a job and had found one as an assistant tailoress. What did Mathew think? Mathew, who was sixteen at the time, replied without hesitation that it was a good idea. He hadn't seen the sense of shame his mother felt at having to "go out to work" to make the family financially viable. Middle class married women did not take paid employment in those days. Why on earth not, asked Mathew when Leah quietly explained how she felt. Without any inculcated prejudice, Mathew saw no problem at all and, when his mother pressed her arguments and fears more strongly, just said that it was nobody else's damn business. Leah, of course, had already signed up for the job but lapped up her son's approval.

Her place of work was in the back rooms of a small gents' outfitter about a mile from home. She could walk there. Leah had never been afraid of work, presumably born of her years as surrogate mother after her own mother died – and before. She quickly found her feet and her knowledge and experience of tailoring learned from her father stood her in good stead. Very soon, she was accepted by all in the back rooms as junior only to the tailor and cutter himself. Leah had led a fairly polite and respectable life, but there came a rude awakening in that workshop. The language used and subjects openly discussed were eye-openers for Leah. But she enjoyed that robust scene immediately. At home with Mathew one evening while they were doing the washing up, she began gently shaking with laughter. Mathew asked what it was all about.

'Oh! One of the girls in the workshop was commenting on the general incompetence of the tailor. She described him as walking around like a fart in a trance,' she said and began giggling all over again. It was quite a revelation for Mathew as well.

Leah grew in that job. She gained so much confidence and self-respect. She hadn't told Arno when she first took the job. She felt unsure of his reaction. But, after a couple of weeks, she told her tale. Arno was very surprised and at a loss for words. But only for a short moment. He grinned with pleasure and began to ask her about her job. He knew something of the tailoring trade himself, of course; he had gleaned that from his father. So he felt comfortable with her choice of work straight away. She was immensely relieved by Arno's open view for she hadn't expected that. Leah didn't mention her job to Honor and Bill when they next shared a Sunday's television and cards. Quite independently, both Mathew and his mum watched Honor closely to see if Arno had spilled the beans but there was no sign.

Something like two months later, Mathew returned home from school to find his mother grinning from ear to ear. She ushered him into the kitchen and gestured towards the oven. To its left sat a small refrigerator. A fridge! She had wanted a fridge for years. She had kept bottles of milk on a marble slab in the pantry. It was probably the coolest room in the house, having only one very small window and that facing north, but in the summer the milk would often start going off and the butter was over-soft. Honor had owned a much larger American fridge for years but never really got on with modern technology so she kept it in the garage because it was too big for the kitchen, and used it at a quarter capacity to store beer which few in her household drank much of. Now Leah had her own! It was only a cheap model and small but it worked and she had bought it all by herself without reference to anyone. My God, was she proud of herself. Mathew was just as proud of his mum and said so. When Arno came home and saw what she had achieved, he was somewhat reserved but quietly pleased with his working wife. Honor and Bill were invited for tea and cards that weekend and shown the new acquisition within minutes of their arrival. Honor was rather astounded and asked why Leah would want a fridge. Mathew jumped in rather brusquely.

'To keep things cold!' he announced. 'Mum bought it from her job earnings.' His father looked at him sharply and he fell silent. Bill said nothing but Leah felt his approval. So that cat was now well and truly out of the bag. There was no explosion. There were sideways looks but nothing was said. After all, the answer to any and all objections was sitting there in the kitchen for all to see.

There was a growing sense of stability in Leah's household after that – a sense of new confidence. It's amazing what a few spare bob can do.

Leah's Triumph

Christmas time came round again. That year, 1955, it was the Baebers' turn to host things on the day. The Dentons would reciprocate on Boxing Day. As ever, Leah and Arno laid on a good show for Christmas lunch. The highly polished reproduction oak table was laid with individual place mats covered with Else's crocheted doilies. Both Else and Frederick had died by this time and Arno had inherited that marvellous crochetry. The cutlery and glassware were shining; each glass had been breathed on by Arno before being given its final polish with a clean, dry cloth. Damask serviettes were carefully folded and placed next to each setting. The meal began, as did all important meals organised by Arno, with Heinz cream of tomato soup. This was followed by roast goose with sage and onion stuffing, Yorkshire puddings, roast potatoes and sprouts – an unbreakable tradition in that household for many years yet and all remarkably reminiscent of Christmas dinners served by Fred and Else in their happier days. Ale was served to everyone, including Mathew and Tony (but they could only have one glass). Christmas pudding brought up the rear. It all took a great effort and Leah was exhausted afterwards. Arno shared many of the day's tasks but Leah took the brunt of the cooking. She always accused Arno of trying to over-impress his guests, regardless of effort, or more to the point, of cost. Those accusations irritated Arno and were a waste of breath but she never stopped making them. Nor were they completely fair, for Arno genuinely liked laying on a spread and doing it right; and Mathew understood that from an early age. He also saw that his mother's complaint was not baseless, for the family had been running on empty financially for many years. This year things were rather easier, though. One family tradition which was not inherited from Arno's childhood was FHB; Mathew learned early on about how Honor and Arno had laughed at the "family hold back" admonition – and, indeed, heard them both laughing at it now. Tony had learned the same story so everyone sang from the same hymn sheet.

On Boxing Day, Honor prepared a splendid cold meal, as she nearly always did, of salmon with potato and green salads. The salmon still came from a tin though. The days of plenty we enjoy today had not yet arrived in that neck of the woods. She had put a large Christmas tree in the corner of the room, bedecked with those wonderful glass decorations which she had inherited from her mother. After everyone chipped in to the clearing and washing up, but before setting out the card table, Honor brought out a book to show her guests. Honor could be susceptible to some odd things. On an earlier occasion, she had shown everybody a book called "Your Fate". It was a compendium of astrological predictions based solely upon one's star sign. Mathew was incredulous of a prediction that his health would centre around his heart and lungs simply because his birthdate defined him as a Gemini. When he had been four and five, he had suffered a very bad cough lasting over a year and been treated by Dr. Haas, the family physician, for chronic bronchitis; so the astrological prediction seemed accurate. He was able to see, however, and indeed strenuously said, that one would have to check whether everyone sharing his astrological sign was similarly afflicted. He got rather excited with this subject and a quite intense argument arose when Mathew told his aunt that it was "stupid" to believe something like that just because it was written in a book. He was rather articulate that day but too immature to know when to be discreet. Honor became rather agitated and Arno was clearly unhappy. Leah sat quietly and said nothing. Bill too remained silent.

Arno hadn't spoken a word as he drove his family home. He stopped at a tobacconist's and got out to buy some cigs. Leah said to Mathew, 'I thought you argued very well,' and when Mathew asked why everyone seemed so upset, she explained to him that his dad and Aunt Honor were very close and when Honor got upset, so would Dad. Mathew had never thought of that before but he understood immediately and connected his mother's remark with many other little things he had noticed over the years. He was, however, pleased with his mother's approval of his line of argument. He was beginning to see that he and his mum had something important in common.

Well, this Boxing Day, Honor showed everyone a book which Tony had borrowed from Hull Library; though nobody explained why he had borrowed it. It was a thick and beautifully printed book about Albert Einstein and his work. There were a very few words in English but the bulk of the book was page after page of dense algebra. 'Isn't it marvellous?' Honor was insisting. Mathew had begun elementary algebra at that stage so understood that x could stand for anything at all but he knew little else. He saw complex symbols all over the pages, often with both subscripts and superscripts but he had absolutely no idea what these might mean. Honor was waxing lyrical about how anyone could write such things but she understood even less than her nephew. Mathew, however, couldn't really comprehend why his aunt should be getting so excited about something neither she nor anyone else in the room had a clue about. It all seemed like a sort of hero-worship without understanding; indeed, her response seemed like some sort of religion to Mathew. He had learned, however, not to verbalise such thoughts and he kept his views to himself until talking it through with his mother later. Nevertheless, he did share Honor's wonderment at this world of abstruse tensor algebra and resolved to try and understand it one day. But that thought was between him and himself.

Time passed. It was the week before Easter when, after washing up the dishes from tea, Leah asked Arno and Mathew to follow her into the lounge. They were somewhat puzzled by this move but did as they were bidden. As soon as they got past the door, they both saw it. Sitting in the corner of the room was a television set. Leah had bought a television set! But, my God! It was exactly – exactly – the same model as that owned by Honor and Bill. Arno was, quite literally, gobsmacked. Mathew understood immediately and grinned from ear to ear. This would show them! Arno asked whether the set was on loan or on hire. No, she insisted, she had bought it outright. No instalments, no hire-purchase – outright. My God, how much was she earning from her job? Just the same as before. She had saved for months, had she not?

They all sat down in front of those shiny, curved walnut-veneered doors and waited to see what was on that evening. Mathew rushed to open the doors and switch on the set. The BBC was showing an *Interlude* called *The Waving Wheat*. It showed waving grass in black and white for a whole ten minutes. They didn't care. They were watching on their own telly Afterwards, the scene changed and a newsreader appeared with the happenings of the day. Mathew was more interested than his parents but everyone kept their seats. Then came an episode of *No Hiding Place*. Great! Arno poured some drinks. Advocaat for him and Mathew, cherry brandy for Leah. They all settled in for a good watch. My God, had life not changed for them? Their evening habits were never the same again.

Honor and Bill had been invited for Easter Sunday tea. Afterwards, everybody repaired to the lounge. When Honor saw the TV set, her eyes nearly popped out of her head.

'Mum bought that from her earnings,' said Mathew, proud as punch.

Arno nodded and did not hide his pride.

Bill caught Leah's eye and he smiled at her with genuine, heartfelt admiration.

It took a further moment before Honor got it.

'It's the same model as ours!'

EXTRA CURRICULAR

Early On

Peter had first met Jonathon in secondary school in 1951. They had both gained scholarships there in the same year. I don't think I should reveal the name of their school lest it acquire a reputation as a hothouse for sedition or something. Let's just say that it was a minor public school in the north of England. Jonathon's family were considerably better off than Peter's but being in the same school trumped all that. Jonathon had attended the private junior school before winning his scholarship, but Peter's parents could never have afforded that sort of thing. Indeed, Peter's background was such that he really had no idea what to expect when he sat down to the Eleven Plus exam and it was regarded as a bloody miracle when he passed well enough to get into what was generally acknowledged as the best school in his home city. When he finally took up his place, he found himself in the B stream of the first seniors' year. Jonathon, with far more savvy parents, had made the A stream. So it wasn't correct of me to say that the boys met in 1951. I should have said that they both entered the senior school in 1951. There, that's better.

Peter really enjoyed his first year in the school and made more friends than he'd ever made before, though none as close as his old mate, Dave. He'd more or less lost contact with David, however, partly because of David's parents' tactics in connection with the Eleven Plus, and partly because of Dave's dad's job. Let me explain. Some months before that fateful examination, parents had been asked to complete a form listing the city's schools in order of preference so far as they were concerned. Their child would be awarded, or not of course, a place as high in that list as his or her marks permitted, subject, of course, to there remaining any places. David's parents felt that a minor public school was socially above their son and, in any case, he wasn't likely to get there. No doubt, it was this last estimation which gave solidity to their anti-social-climbing stance. However, as they say in all the best stories, David was a sight more able than his parents imagined and would have certainly won a place at that minor public school. Instead, he ended up at the grammar school. To be fair, it was a good school but provided a lesser chance in life than the minor public school. Let us not be coy about these things, eh? However, just before David took up his place at the grammar, his father's bosses moved him to a posting in Liverpool. That was the end of the earth so far as David and Peter were concerned. Peter did visit David in his new home in due course, but their friendship dwindled to a beautiful memory after that. So any new friends that Peter made in his new school were a boon.

I'll tell you about just one of them. His name was Piddington. I forgot to say, by the way, that this was a boys-only school, so girls won't get a look-in in this story – nor, Peter was sad to say, in his early life either. Peter never knew his first name; the boys never used first names, you know. Piddington was a big boy for his age – big and round, and as jolly as that sketch might suggest. He sat at a desk in the adjacent row to Peter, immediately next to him. Apart from the many occasions when they would share a crafty smirk or a telling put-down as near-neighbours, their proximity was virtually essential to their main trade. Let me set the scene.

That class of theirs was assigned a Mr. Forsyth as French master. Frankly, it was amazing that any boy in L3B learned any French at all and that's not only because Forsyth was a lousy teacher. The real problem was that he had a unique style of man management. If any boy spoke out of turn – and that could quite easily just have been to ask the teacher for a translation (mind you, don't be fooled by descriptions like that; those boys could be very crafty and provocative) – he would give out "lines" on the spot.

'Fifty lines, Piddlington,' he would snap, with deliberate mispronunciation and for the boys' great hilarity. Should Piddington demur, Forsyth would amend his punishment, 'Hundred lines, Piddlington.'

Mr. Forsyth had been a captain or something in the army during the war and sometimes his fellow teachers would actually use the handle. But not the boys. Their piercing scrutiny of Mr. Forsyth's sleek, combed-back, jet-black hair and his equally jet-black pencil moustache, rolled into perfectly straight, long points at the end, together with his generally flamboyant behaviour, led them, with that delicious discernment which only schoolboys can create, to the sobriquet, "Flash". A little alliteration helped as well. So it was that when Flash Forsyth distributed lines like confetti, the class resolved to find a defence.

They hit upon the idea of writing lines like, "I must behave properly in class" and similarly lofty jousts at literature, in advance. Since, in no time at all, every boy in the class was given fifty or a hundred lines by Flash Forsyth – and many times over too – every young lad was willing to do his bit for the cause. Piddington was assigned to collect and store the aforesaid lines in his desk, ready for immediate distribution when the call came.

'Fifty lines, boy,' roared Flash, and in a trice, the offending monster would proffer a small sheaf, comprising fifty repeats of some masterful literary mantra. Forsyth was ever fair. He accepted whatever was offered without fail. He never questioned where the lines had come from nor did he look at what was written or in which hand. It was all frightfully decent and efficient.

At the end of the year, Flash Forsyth, who was also the form master, by the way, announced – or, more accurately, it was announced for him a couple of days earlier by the headmaster (otherwise known as The Boss to all six-hundred-odd pupils in the school) – that he was retiring and that their last day of term would be his very last day at the school also. While Flash Forsyth had never provoked any real sense of idolatry or admiration from his class, nobody felt any animus towards the old spiv. It took but a moment's collaborative discussion for the class to come up with a suitable marking of his passing. Without anything being said, one by one, each of the thirty-odd pupils of Lower Three B stood and marched up to their form-master's desk, placed fifty, a hundred, or even two hundred lines upon it and returned whence he came. Flash quietly watched the procession with a gleeful grin slowly growing over his chops. When all were done, he scooped up the truly immense piles of lines into his bag and made a short bow. What a very civilised school, Peter, thought; this is what education is really about.

Oh, dear me! I have wandered off the point a little but I simply had to get all that off my chest. What I had wanted to say was that Peter did very good work in all subjects in his first year – even gaining a decent fourth place in French, would you believe – and was promoted to the A stream as a result. So was Piddington, which pleased Peter a lot. When next year came round, they found themselves in U3A under the tender care of Mr. Bower, the school's senior Latin master. And it was in that class that Peter first met Jonathon who, as I said earlier, had been placed in L3A from the beginning. Peter and Jonathon took to each other early on, and daily after lunch, would stroll around the school grounds together, grounds which, by the way, were quite beautiful because, way back, the school had been built within the city's former botanical gardens. All around the perimeter were handsome, tall horse-chestnut trees, interplanted with glorious rhododendron bushes. As they walked, Peter and Jonathon would talk about so many different things: science, which was their favourite subject; fine art and what they then understood as culture – jokes; and the masters – usually in the same breath – and politics. Jonathon, by the way, was a handsome lad, with well-groomed black hair, who always dressed very neatly. His dad was an engineer who, Peter learned later, had worked on radar during the war. At the time, of course, Peter had no idea at all what an engineer was, let alone radar, but Jonathon was obviously proud of his father and that was good enough for Peter. Peter's dad had a very modest job so they didn't talk about that. Undoubtedly, Peter felt in some awe of Jonathon's background but that, of course, was half the point of attending a minor public school, was it not?

It was at U3A's year's end when Peter's education advanced by another great step. The ritual had arisen in that minor public school of form masters reading out the names of all pupils within their charge, to be answered by each lad identifying (confessing?) the source of his financial support.

'Buggins!'

"City council" might be the reply, or "County council" for those pupils living in the countryside around that town.

If neither of these, the reply would be, "Payee". That meant that the lad was in the school by dint of his parent's wealth, rather than by having won a free place in the Eleven Plus examination and so paid for by the town or county councils. Peter could never understand, by the way, why the response was *payee* rather than *payer*, but he was given to such pedantry. The distribution of pupils amongst these three possibilities was, broadly speaking: A stream, all scholarship boys; B stream, around half scholarship and half payee; C stream, usually all payee. The boys' summary of these statistics was as unsophisticated as it was cruel: "Brights in A or B, thickos in C".

The whole process of question and answer took a good ten minutes. Every boy in U3A answered "Citycouncil" or "County council", until it came to Piddington.

'Payee,' he replied, without embarrassment.

Peter was astonished, for Piddington was demonstrably one of the cleverer lads in the class. Peter thought about this for a few moments before the truth dawned on him.

Just because your parents are rich, doesn't mean that you're thick.

He never forgot that lesson although he did find more elegant ways to express it in later life. Education in life need not be confined to a syllabus.

We might wonder today, by the way, at the crass insensitivity of requiring pupils publicly to announce the source of their financial support, but those were different times.

Anyway, as the years rushed by, Peter's work went reasonably well, as did Jonathon's and they each passed in a fair number of subjects at 'O' level when the time came at the end of their year in the fifth form. That was the time when pupils could leave school for good to make their way in the big, wide world, or to continue into the sixth and to specialise with the longer-term expectation of going to university. Both Peter and Jonathon joined the science sixth form, something that Peter had looked forward to for years. Although he had managed well enough in his arts subjects, he had always looked forward to dropping them and pursuing his great loves in the science world. He had really shone in chemistry, physics and maths so he was set to go. Jonathon had been somewhat broader in his mastery of the large 'O' level syllabus but without the shine of any top position even in his preferred science subjects. He had easily done well enough, though, and had his sights set on becoming some sort of engineer, like his father. Peter, on the other hand, had absolutely no idea what he wanted to be and didn't really know what a university was.

But he was about to enjoy himself!

Right at that time when the world was seemingly about to open its doors wide for him, disaster struck. Peter had been routinely examined by chest X-ray three years earlier and found to have a small degree of tubercular infection. Now, however, another routine check-up showed that the disease had spread and he was to take to his bed for six months and be treated with a cocktail of three drugs. He learned from his specialist much later that he had been lied to in that it was expected that he would be bedridden for at least two years. In the event, the wonder drugs did their thing and Peter was allowed back into school after just eight months. He had been very lucky, but he didn't really see things that way at the time. He rejoined the sixth form with boys formally from the year behind. Of course that didn't matter in the long run but he had to make new friends and re-establish himself. However, he was now studying his favourite subjects and doing very well. He lost contact with Jonathon, unfortunately, which was a shame but not a disaster.

After two years, Peter sat his 'A' level exams and did well enough to win a state scholarship. He hung on for a third year in the sixth form to try for a place or better in Oxford or Cambridge but was unsuccessful. He was very disappointed but went on to a moderately sparkling career later. But that is not our story. Once more, I have allowed myself to be distracted by the background. I am so sorry. Well, maybe not for I have a couple of other tales to tell of Peter's learning things not to be found in the curriculum.

High Fidelity

One day while Peter and Jonathon were still together in the fifth form, Jonathon spoke about hi-fi. Peter had absolutely no idea what he was talking about. So began a lengthy explanation of good quality music reproduction and all that kind of thing. Jonathon backed it up by inviting Peter to his home to listen to the system owned by his father, the electrical engineer. His dad wasn't at home at the time so the boys had the drawing room all to themselves. The amplifier was made by the Leak company. Jonathon explained how they not only designed their circuits with subtle skill but that they selected their components with great care so that they fulfilled the design specifications as near-exactly as possible. At that time, Leak amplifiers were the best money could buy. Coupled to that amplifier, Jonathon's father had set up two wonderful speakers with superb bass response and, at the input end, a state of the art turntable and pickup. Peter was dazzled by all this technology and waffle. Jonathon began to demonstrate the system by playing Rimsky-Korsakov's *Scheherazade*, music which Peter had never heard before. He was bowled over by the demonstration. He had never before heard such detailed and luscious sounds. It was a revelation and in later years, Peter acquired a top-rank hi-fi set of his own, but he never forgot that awakening. Later in the afternoon, Jonathon played a recording of *West Side Story*, a new American musical which had only just come to London. Peter's education was broadening by the minute.

Then, as we know, Peter and Jonathon parted ways because of Peter's hiatus caused by TB. After Peter's return to school, his musical experience blossomed in two quite different ways, which both grew out of a quite unrelated fact. That was Peter's finding a new friend who lived in the same street and with whom he often shared a bus ride home from school. Unusually for schoolboys, especially at his school, he only got to know his new friend by his forename, Denis. Somehow his surname never came up. Anyway, the thing Peter learned about from Denis was that there was a rowing club nearby. Denis asked Peter if he'd like to see it and maybe join. Peter had never liked sport of any kind and his instinct was to refuse the offer but Denis explained that it was more like a social club than a rowing club. If you wanted to row, you could; if not, you were welcome to hang around and just meet everybody. So Peter agreed to be shown the place, which was immediately beyond a couple of fields behind his home. The clubhouse was a substantial, brick-built, two-storey building right on the river bank. It had been there many years, and indeed, Peter had often cycled past it and wondered what it was for; so now he knew. It was pretty dilapidated and the rowing activity had been resurrected only recently. The river was windy and rather narrow for such activities so no eights were rowed on it. But there were plenty of fours, pairs and single sculls. Not that Peter knew any of these terms right then. He had thought of rowing boats as those tubs on local park lakes.

He went along to the club and met a few young people with whom he found common ground, and in due course, he began to cox. He knew little about the sport but surprised himself by getting really interested in the competitions the rowers were entering. On one weekend, he joined in on a trip to Nottingham to witness a contest known as the *Head of the Trent*, referring to the River Trent which runs through that fine old city. Rowers from his club actually did quite well. Peter shouted himself hoarse as he joined in with the other club supporters. That trip probably marked the beginning of a major turnaround in Peter's life, for prior to his joining that club, he had been a happy but fairly solitary soul; thereafter, he became gregarious and quite unable to live without others' company. Socially, the rowing club was a godsend but it did take up a great deal of Peter's time. He joined a band. He had no skill with any instrument but he could pull the string of a tea-chest bass in time with whatever tunes were being played by a Bud Roe on trumpet and a Michael Chamberlain on clarinet. Skiffle was all the rage at that time. Then he borrowed a ukulele and Bud showed him how to form a few basic chords. Later he bought a guitar and taught himself a few more chords and learned to pick out a few tunes but he never learned to read music. He was, let us say, enthusiastic. Nobody worried about the amateurish performances while having an occasional drink at the club. It was the girls who focussed the lads' minds at that time. Bud's girlfriend,

Elizabeth, was extremely attractive and all the boys adored her. But she was Bud's so nobody pushed in. She and Bud, whose real name by the way was Dave, loved dancing so it was natural that there came a call for a dance to be organised at the club one Saturday evening. Liz, her younger sister Anne and several other girls set to and made some cakes, tarts and such things, the bar was well-stocked with soft drinks (the club captain forbade alcohol as the club had no licence), the upper room of the club set atop the changing room was swept clean and generally tarted up and softly lit with oil lamps on the walls, and generally, every little thing was made welcoming for the night. Peter had never experienced an occasion like this before in his sheltered life. He relished it.

 He went early to the club when Saturday evening came. He was one of the organisers and wanted to check that everything was tickety-boo. It was. In due course, people came and the band struck up. Peter did his bit and enjoyed himself enormously, as did everyone else as far as he could tell. After a lengthy stint with his horn, Bud wanted to have a break and a drink with Liz. Peter got himself a drink and wandered out onto a balcony from where rowing addicts in former and more splendiferous times would watch races. There he spotted a solitary girl and thought he'd try his luck for the very first time in his life. It took an enormous act of courage for him even to approach her. But it all started very well. She seemed to be a nice, quiet girl, willing to talk and who knew? Maybe more. Peter suggested that they go for a walk around the fields surrounding the club and she agreed. Peter's heart began to pump a little harder. Well, to tell the truth, it was in his mouth. Outside it was the beginning of a long dusk. The grass in the fields was quite long – half-way up their calves. It was also WET. Peter had the intelligence to realise that this was no environment conducive to a passionate snog, and certainly not for the grope he had hoped to progress to. He did not have, unfortunately, the skill or experience to stop himself trying, to walk instead along the paths, however public, and settle for something less. By the time they had completed a circuit in the dank grass, his chosen mate had sopping wet stockings, was well and truly pissed off and was desirous of an immediate change of beau. Peter had completely lost his bottle, felt foolish and was completely aware of the prat he was. He knew that he had just had an important lesson in life; he was less sure just what that lesson was. In one way, however, he got away with it in that nobody was around to witness his humiliation, or as he only came to realise much later, the girl's humiliation either. In later life, Peter found many other ways to make a fool of himself. Each time he was convinced that his feelings were original.

Ah well! All that didn't stop Peter becoming ever closer friends with Michael, the clarinet player. Actually, Mike was a most attractive boy, to boys as well as girls. Nothing remotely deviant is intended here; Mike was completely heterosexual. It's just that he had a way with him such that folk couldn't help but like and be attracted to him. Peter saw it completely and was envious but that didn't prevent their forming a strong bond. That bond was cemented by jazz. Mike had a fair collection of modern jazz records and a record player. Peter had neither but had always responded well to almost any sort of music although his experience in that area was almost as dire as his experience in sex. He and Mike fell into the habit of meeting alternately in their family homes, which were only a street apart, almost every evening in school holidays to talk, to drink their fathers' whisky eked out with endless coffees, and to play Mike's wonderful collection of modern jazz. They would begin around seven in the evening and whoever was the guest would depart for home in the wee small hours. Their conversation would cover every conceivable topic, even politics, but mostly art in one form or another.

Peter had heard quite a few trad jazz pieces over the years but this modern jazz stuff was amazing to him. At first, he found it somewhat difficult, but he got it after a while and became a true convert. Gerry Mulligan, MJQ (which Mike explained was an abbreviation for the Modern Jazz Quartet, as everyone knew) and Bobby Brookmeyer were their staples, and of course, Mike's collection, though interesting, wasn't large, so every one of his records was played repeatedly during their months together. Later on, Mike suddenly appeared with a completely new record which he was champing to play to Peter. Not music for music's sake this time. It was the first LP – a ten inch disk – put out by Tom Lehrer. What sophistication! What hilarity! After many playings, Peter and Michael memorised all the lyrics to *I'll Hold Your Hand in Mine*. Not an easy feat. They were in hysterics with their achievement. It was a wonderful summer for Peter. It wasn't to be repeated, unfortunately, because Mike was one year ahead of Peter (that hiatus all over again) and while Peter continued on to his final year in the sixth form, Mike went off to Newcastle University to read medicine. They met a couple of times after that but only briefly.

Well, that was fun, wasn't it? I've let myself get distracted once more because the reason why I got into all of this was to relate that Peter decided one day to build his own hi-fi system. Well, it wasn't hi-fi and Peter knew that full well, but at least, it had power. He bought a kit for a small public-address amplifier and put it all together in no time at all. He also bought a large speaker cone. Again, it wasn't hi-fi because he couldn't afford hi-fi but it was large, about twelve inches across, and Peter made a large cabinet for it, one with castors and a handle so that he could cart it around if need be. He also bought an inexpensive turntable and pickup so as to complete his own record playing kit. No, it wasn't hi-fi but it was many times better and certainly very many more times more powerful than Mike's little Dansette. He bought himself a few LPs and of course, these included some Gerry Mulligan jazz and some MJQ, different recordings to those he had memorised with Mike. So now, just about the time that Mike departed for Newcastle, Peter had a system of his own.

He mentioned his achievement to various friends at school, not to brag, simply to inform and maybe seek out other boys who might be interested in music. It worked, but his new friend came from an entirely unexpected quarter.

Two French Masters

Peter was approached after school one day by Mr. Mitchell, one of the French teachers. Mo Mitchell, as he was known to all the boys, had the reputation of being a fairly quiet man, and a good teacher who was reasonably popular and respected. And schoolboys should know these things. He wasn't known to Peter because *his* French lessons had been given by a quite different man about whom there is another charming story. Here I go again! I shall interrupt myself straight away with this tale from Peter's school life in the fourth form.

His French teacher that year, Mr. O'Dell, was a kind but efficient young man who taught well and had an easy grip on his charges. He encouraged pupils to speak French at every opportunity. One day, he used the lesson as a simple quiz. He spoke, in careful French, about his colleagues. He asked the class to identify one of their teachers who, he explained, was known for his rather large backside. The boys were stupidly amazed to think that any teacher would be aware of their nicknames for the masters. In this particular case, the chemistry master, who had a very large backside and who emphasised the fact by walking along with his hands thrust out sideways in the pockets of his loose trousers, was called Mr. Dennis. Mr. O'Dell suggested that his initials were R.C. Indeed, the boys' nickname for Mr. Dennis was "Arsey". At one point, Mr. O'Dell said to the class, 'My name's O'Dell, so get that into your noddles.' His nickname was "Oddel". Mr. O'Dell was a most popular master.

Well, somehow, one of the boys in Peter's class discovered that Oddel was about to get married. He'd probably learnt that from his parents' knowing Mr. O'Dell but that's by the way. Anyway, word got round the class in a trice, as you'd expect, and it was decided that Derick Nurse, the most able speaker of French in the class, would give a little speech of felicitation, in French of course, at the beginning of the next lesson with Mr. O'Dell. When that moment came and Oddel had just about opened his mouth to begin the lesson, Nurse stood up near the back of the class-room and began to spout in French. Haltingly certainly, but Peter and his friends were able to follow most of what was being said. So was Oddel. As it slowly dawned on him what Nurse was saying, he sank slowly to his knees on the dais at the front, holding his hands together at his mouth as if in prayer, while he listened to every last word in that beautiful little speech. Nurse offered Mr. O'Dell the felicitations of the class on his engagement and upcoming marriage… and so on and so forth. For Peter it was one of the most moving moments he had ever witnessed. When Derick finished his short oration, the whole class burst into rapturous applause. Young boys of thirteen to fourteen can be surprisingly sensitive.

Well that was all about a different French master, as I said. So we're back to Mo Mitchell. Mo and his wife, Laura, enjoyed a charming little hobby together, namely country dancing. Not square dancing as in America but a rather more quiet and genteel pastime which has been around, certainly in Britain, for hundreds of years. Mo, together with a couple of friends, provided the music for the dancing and Laura "called", which is to say that she called out the steps, particularly to beginners of whom there were plenty. Mo was looking for amplification for his wife's calling. Somehow or other, he had heard that Peter had a powerful amplifier and speaker system. Would Peter like to join the band and bring his amplification system along? Peter was flattered to be asked by one of his school's teachers and felt that he'd be joining in something a little more grown-up than his other activities. He had bought an electric pick-up for his guitar by this time and so looked forward to picking out the odd tune here and there. The stalwarts of Mo's band were Mo on accordion, Mona on piano, and Les on drums, mostly snare. Mo was insistent that Peter play quiet chords for most of the time and which Mo wrote on the music for him, but allowed him to pick out short front-line phrases occasionally. Peter understood completely why Mo gave these directions. It wasn't only because of Peter's limited musical skills – which were as evident to Peter as they were to the rest of the band – but also because an over-enthusiastic use of electric guitar wouldn't blend well at all with the well-established country style of the music these people were playing. Peter never once overstepped the mark. Mo's wife was pleased to be amplified and Mo's band were pleased enough to accommodate a young interloper.

There would be a dance organised most weekends. Mo would pick Peter up in his large hatchback wagon near his home and load up the large speaker box, amplifier and guitar in the back and off they would drive to some village or other several miles outside the city. Mostly, their dances were held in a village hall or, if the weather was very kind, on a village green – provided, of course, they were within the cables' reach of a power point. Catchy pieces with memorable titles like *Muckin' i' George's Byre* were the stuff of their sophisticated country dancing experiences. This, Peter mused ironically (*not* sarcastically, for it was all only a bit of fun, after all), was high living! In one village hall venue, the band's only access to the stage was *via* the gents. Laura was terribly embarrassed to be taken past the porcelain in that holy of holies.

The highlight venue for the group, however, was in a large barn owned by some wealthy farmer about thirty miles out of town. He had arranged to have cleared a large area of tidied earth and had spread around several bales of pristine hay to be used as seats, and when arranged in different ways, as side tables. Oil lamps were scattered around to provide a quite wonderful old-fashioned, country atmosphere. A bar was provided with free drinks for all and small glasses loaded up with cigarettes were distributed around the hay bales. Peter, availing himself of both cigs and booze, looked across at Mo. Mo, who was, let's face it, *in loco parentis*, just said to Peter, 'Don't overdo it, Peter,' and carried on with his chain smoking.

Peter thought that was very civilised of him. He was, in any case, not the sort of boy to take undue advantage. But he did enjoy himself that evening.

Some of Life's Little Coincidences

Well, the day came when Peter took the train to London to begin his university career. He had won a place to read chemistry at Imperial College in South Kensington. He had found somewhere to live in South Ken itself, which was most fortunate as most students not billeted in college accommodation had to find quarters many tube stops away. Peter was to live in a flat in Drayton Gardens, a mere quarter-hour's walk into The Royal College of Science, one of the three constituent colleges of Imperial. The flat was rented by a Mr. and Mrs. Brittian and they were subletting three rooms of the large apartment to students as a way of paying their own way. Peter had never been thrust into the close company of others before and was apprehensive at meeting four cohabitants. Nothing new there, of course, but hindsight and experience are wonderful things.

Mrs. Brittian introduced Peter to his flatmates as they appeared. First was John Cornwell, a boy from his old school, would you believe. Peter knew him only vaguely because Cornwell was from the arts side of life and, as Charles Snow had famously insisted several years earlier: never the twain shall meet. Furthermore, Cornwell was a rugby player and Peter had never got on with anything so physical or groupie. Throughout the coming months, Cornwell would take off for a morning or evening run around the local streets and park as a way of keeping fit. Trouble was, he came back so stinking of sweat that both Peter and all his fellows had to remonstrate with him. 'John – take a shower for God's sake!' was the cry.

Cornwell was to read literature at University College, which was across town in Bloomsbury. Apart from his olfactory problems, John Cornwell turned out to be a good flatmate, always seeking middle ground in any dispute.

Then came Jeff Stibbins, who was to read physics at Imperial. He was a pleasant enough bloke but had no prior connection to Peter or anyone else in the group.

Joe Redland, a diminutive guy, reading history at University College, was similarly unknown to anyone else. He was a gregarious man, from whom Peter was to learn a thing or two, as we shall see. The last of his fellow cohabitants was an utter surprise and delight.

It was none other than Peter's old childhood friend David, whose family had gone to Liverpool. Dave was to read economics and sociology at the London School of Economics in the Strand. Peter and David chose to share a room for the duration. They spent a fair time together, much of it in South Kensington coffee bars. None of the group drank in pubs much, possibly to eke out their grants. However things turned out for them in later life, they began pretty clean.

OK. So there we have the set up. Five young men starting on their roads to God knows where, each in his way, perhaps a little more frightened of the prospect than he would ever admit. It wasn't long, however, before Joe Redland unpacked a record player, much to Peter's delight. Peter hadn't brought his cumbersome record player with him but he missed those evenings with Mike Chamberlain listening to modern jazz. Anyway, here was a new friend who had the necessary equipment. *His* preference was for classical music. That was fine by Peter though, and he was avid to learn. Many evenings were spent listening to Joe's collection. Dave had some LPs of Kenneth McKeller, which John Cornwell adored. Peter was less enamoured. Later in their first term, Joe came back with a new record. It was of a piece he had been talking about for weeks: Stravinsky's *Rite of Spring*. What a revelation! Peter did not react like those Frenchmen had in Paris when the *Rite* was first performed, however. Maybe he might have, had he been immersed in the more traditional classical music as they no doubt were, but I doubt it. He took to it like a duck to water, so much so that his fellow residents got fed up to the back teeth with his incessant playing of Joe's record. Peter was to remember Joe for the rest of his life for that exposure to new music.

He remembered him for something else, too. Poker. Oh dear! Not a good idea to play poker at the best of times but certainly not when all your worldly wealth is expressed within a ninety-five pounds a term grant. Peter had been reluctant to play for that very reason, but fear of being churlish made him yield eventually. Make no mistake though, Joe was no card sharp. In that pastime, Joe was an idiot. It all began with Joe explaining the rules of the game. So you have the picture? The blind leading the blind. They agreed to play for very modest increments, no raise more than sixpence being acceptable. After they had been playing for about an hour, Peter noticed that Joe was bluffing on every other hand. As regular as clockwork. Peter had never been especially sharp at cards but realised full well what to do! After two pleasurable hours, listening all the while to Schubert and his friends, Peter was twenty-five pounds up. He came to his senses and realised just how high a proportion of the term's grant that represented. He suggested that they stop and give all the money back.

'We've had a lot of fun but this is ridiculous,' he said.

Joe would have none of it. A debt was a debt… or some such code of honour. So they began again. Joe continued with his winning strategy and his losses continued to mount. Then Peter realised that he could simply alter the phase of his own play and so use Joe's strategy to his (Joe's) advantage; Joe's position gradually improved. Peter began to feel an awful lot better. But then, goddammit, Joe changed his strategy to something Peter couldn't unravel, and began to lose again. Peter struggled manfully until they agreed to call it a night. Joe was down five pounds and insisted on honouring his debt. Still that was a lot better, Peter thought, than twenty-five or more. Peter used his winnings to buy a recording of Schubert's *Great C major* symphony. He repeatedly played that until there were protests, but it was a quieter piece than the *Rite*, at least. More to the point, Peter resolved never to play poker or any other gambling game again and he never did. Education is a wonderful thing, don't you think? In later years, the lotteries came along but that was just like his father doing the pools, wasn't it? That didn't count.

You know, I keep interrupting myself. I am so sorry. I had wanted to mention something quite unexpected which happened to Peter on his third day in the Big City. He had decided to go across town to the main Students' Union building in Bloomsbury near University College. As he walked towards Russell Square, he came to a road junction and saw a tightly-furled umbrella jerk up as its owner flourished his emblem of state as he was about to turn the corner. Actually, he did more than just see it; he walked into the damn thing. And who should have been swinging that brolly with suave gait but Peter's old friend, Jonathon! Jonathon had always had a penchant for putting on the dog and he had completely mastered the furled umbrella. The two young men greeted each other like the long lost friends they were and Jonathon suggested that they go off for a coffee in a nearby café.

Jonathon, you remember, had been contemporary with Peter before Peter's hiatus with TB. He had won a place at Imperial College's City & Guilds College to read chemical engineering. He was now beginning his second year, of course, so was something of an old hand at this student game. Peter was keen to learn from him.

A Mate on the Right

Actually, it was really only when Peter began his second year at Imperial that he and Jonathon really began to re-form, and indeed, grow their friendship. That was because they both ended up in Beit Hall, one of Imperial College's Halls of Residence on the central site. Right next door to The Royal Albert Hall actually. By the way, I haven't told you about their professional lives; about how well they were doing. I'll tell you why that is. It's because it's a bit boring, because it has little to do with the present tale, and finally, because Peter had not maintained the glory of his school days. He was in line to get his degree in due course, he felt (and he was right), but he was showing none of his former sparkle. Jonathon was probably doing better but he never had harboured hopes of a First. Like Peter, he got a good degree in the end but neither knew that at that time.

One afternoon early in their first term, Alan, an engineering friend of Jonathon's, walked in on them in Jonathon's room, one flight of stairs up from Peter's. They convinced him, that afternoon, that they were utterly mad. Permit me to explain. The students' rooms in Beit Hall were cleaned once a week by a couple of worthy ladies called Maud and Julie. They were a comely pair who were everything you would expect for ladies looking after university students. They were efficient and totally uninterested in their jobs but liked students well enough. Anyway, mid-morning was their time for a cuppa and when one of them had put the kettle on and wanted the other to join her from whichever floor she was working on, she would call out in a bird-like way.

'Julie!' You know, 'Ju-lie!'

'Maud,' the latter almost sung into two syllables.

'Julie, Ma-ud!' And so on, and on, and on. Their calls could be heard all over that wing of the Beit Hall, which was, of course, the idea.

Jonathon and Peter found these avian cries amusing and when Alan called on them that afternoon, he found them, sitting in chairs opposite one another, calling out at the tops of their voices, 'Ju-lie, Ma-ud. Jul-ie, Ma-ud. Ju-lie, Ma-ud.'

They had been doing this for well over half an hour without a break, they told him later. They were feeling so unutterably bored that they could think of nothing else to do. They looked at him as he opened the door, finished their short roundelay and said, without any explanation at all, 'Let's go out for a cup of tea and a bun.'

Peter later claimed that afternoon as some sort of pinnacle of scholastic experience.

He and Jonathon did pursue other matters, you will be pleased to hear. Jonathon had joined the College Conservative Club. I think they liked the alliteration. Alan was the leader of that group of worthies. It was a very small group actually, which is hardly surprising really, given that students of that age are most likely to be on the left side of politics. But not all. Alan was a large chap, a little rotund and quietly-spoken. He exuded a quiet air of effortless confidence which derived, as night follows day, from one of the major public schools of our beloved realm. It was unsurprising that Jonathon should have befriended Alan. It was a tad less clear why Peter should have joined the club. Not that he was a socialist, mind you. Rather that he had no real idea of what he was. He joined the club when he was asked, simply because Jonathon was his mate. He attended just one meeting where politics were discussed, found it all too boring for words and never went to a meeting again. He did, however, join Jonathon and Alan in the bar and coffee bar for their society. Alan was totally uninterested in whether Peter was politically active. Truth to tell, it wasn't completely clear whether Alan himself cared one jot for the club of which he had been elected president. After all, a membership of around six students hardly suggests any feverish adherence to the cause. No, these boys were just having a little social fun.

Keep an Eye Open

Some months later, Jonathon caught Peter's attention one morning and breathlessly urged him to go for a coffee, not that Peter needed much persuasion.

'I must tell,' Jonathon began, 'but in the strictest confidence. You must never say a word about this to anyone.'

Peter gave his assurance.

'Someone's been following me for the last few weeks. I kept seeing this guy in the near distance in various places. It was creepy. After a while, I marched up to him very quickly and challenged him. He didn't appear surprised. In fact, I think he'd made himself obvious deliberately,' he began.

'Sounds odd to me,' Peter said.

'Wait,' continued Jonathon. 'He suggested we go for a coffee as he had an offer to make. We went round to that little café in Gloucester Road; you know, the one which sells those wonderful cheesecakes. Anyway, when he got round to business, he told me that he'd been observing me for several weeks. I told him I knew that but he replied that he'd been doing it for a lot longer than I'd seen him; that he'd let me see him in the end so as to make his approach.'

'This is all cloak and dagger, Jonathon. Very melodramatic!' observed Peter. 'Weren't you a bit wary of all this?'

'I most certainly was and was itching to get out of there but he sensed my, well fear really, and made every effort to calm me down. He said, "Look – don't be nervous. I chose this place to meet so that you wouldn't feel threatened. Please hear me out". He was very well spoken. A really quite posh accent,' continued Jonathon.

Coming from Jonathon, who was well-spoken himself, that was quite a compliment; and Peter could see how that might appeal to his friend.

'Well,' continued Jonathon, 'and this is where it all gets frightfully exciting and scary, he introduced himself as… but I won't mention his name, Peter. I'm sure you'll understand. Anyway, he went on to say that he was a member of our secret service. MI5 or MI6, I guess, but he didn't actually mention the branch. He said that his office was looking at university students all over Britain so as to nip in the bud any subversives before things got out of hand. They were particularly interested in any likely communists.'

'So what has all that got to do with you?' interrupted Peter.

'Wait! Listen. He went on to say that he and his colleagues were looking for student leaders with what they saw as impeccable right-wing credentials to keep an eye out for any likely-looking communists within the student body.'

'You mean to be spies,' interrupted Peter again, ever the one to reduce matters to basics. And he did succeed for a moment, for Jonathon actually paused in his ever more enthusiastic account of the spook.

'Yes, well I know; there is that. But this guy reminded me about that Cambridge spy ring led by Kim Philby and insisted that they were concerned not to let anything like that happen again. The only way they could hope to do that, he said, was to keep close tabs on potential traitors and spies wherever and whenever. He went on to say that their extended observations had persuaded them that I was on side. A loyal, dependable and intelligent man who could be very useful to them in seeking out any student of dubious mien.'

'How did you respond?' asked Peter.

'Well, I agreed, although I had no real idea of where to start. He said that they understood that and would give me pointers from time to time for me to follow up.'

'You mean some people to spy on?' snorted Peter.

Jonathon did not like that at all and protested that he would only look at any suspects from afar. Peter was rather unimpressed but said nothing.

Jonathon continued. 'He suggested that we meet once a week to compare notes. Our first meeting would be when he would buy me lunch in the Dorchester Hotel, would you believe.' The Dorchester was one of the swankiest hotels in London at that time; it still is.

Peter's eyes opened wide and he certainly felt some pangs of jealousy at the mention of that place. 'When is your first meeting?' he asked.

'Oh, we've already had two,' replied Jonathon. 'That one was last week and our second was today.'

'In the Dorchester again?' asked Peter, somehow trying to torture himself.

'Not this time,' replied Jonathon. 'Today we went to Simpson's in The Strand.' Peter knew that Simpson's was one of the great places to eat roast beef in London. His gastric juices were beginning to work overtime. For God's sake, he thought, that would probably cost me twenty percent of my term's grant to eat lunch there! 'We're meeting again next week,' said Jonathon. 'I don't know where yet. He says he'll give me a call during the week to fix it up.'

'Has he given you any names yet?' asked Peter.

'Not yet. He's getting some ready, he says.'

'Sounds like a great lunch club to me,' replied Peter. 'You're a lucky bugger,' and then, as an afterthought, he added, 'I think.'

Meanwhile, desultory meetings of the College Conservative Club were held and when Jonathon and Alan left to join Peter in the bar, a few pints were disposed of in traditional fashion. Jonathon never spoke of his spook friend there, however, and it was clear to Peter that Alan had not been told of him. For his part, Peter gave little attention to searching for reds under his bed for, by that stage in his education, he had discovered far more fun on top of it.

Who Guards the Guards?

While all this excitement was going on, Peter was closing in on his second year's examinations and Jonathon was coming up to the end of his third, but not final, year. The difference arose because the chemical engineering degree took four years and the chemistry degree, three. Another difference arose out of the nature of the chemistry degree which Imperial College quite uniquely offered in those days. May I be permitted to educate *you*, dear reader? Before the First World War, Germany produced scores of chemists qualified to PhD level – far more than did Britain. Those highly qualified chemists helped establish a world-beating chemicals industry in their home country. Forward-thinking politicians in Britain were greatly concerned. They got the message alright and began to persuade British universities to beat the Germans at their own game. At Oxford, chemistry students took four years to finish their BSc course. The first three years were filled with lectures and tutorials, reading and exams. Then, in the fourth year, students would devote all their time to research, leading to what Oxford defined as an honours degree. After that, those interested and talented enough would carry on to a DPhil degree, which was expected to take three years. In other words, seven years from leaving school to a doctorate. Other universities around Britain, including Cambridge, omitted the fourth-year undergraduate research year and so raised doctors in six years. That extra research year in Oxford, however, meant that their DPhils had twenty-five per cent more research experience than students from other establishments. Imperial College, uniquely within London University and possibly the whole country, opted for a different path for chemists (but only for chemists because that's where the urgent need had been identified). There, students would complete the first part of their bachelor chemistry degrees, meaning the lecture/exam part of it all, in just two years; their third year would be given over to research in the style of the Oxford fourth year. One way or another, Britain produced PhDs two or three years sooner than did Germany. The plan succeeded brilliantly if the aim had been simply to produce the youngest PhDs, but in chemistry at Imperial, the cost was a pressure-cooker of a course and without doubt, less well-rounded graduates at the end of the day.

Well, you wanted to know all that, didn't you? The point of the tale, however, is to explain why Peter's second-year examinations were so important. They would be the last exams he would ever take! His final classification would be determined by them and equally, by the quality of research he did in his third year. Despite a brilliantly successful school record in chemistry, Peter had not done at all well at Imperial. The reasons are of no importance to our story, however. What *is* important is that he was getting excited at having exams behind him and beginning research in a new subject he had found and with a research supervisor he admired, but at the same time, shitting himself at the prospect of oncoming failure. Peter's mind was in a turmoil at that time. All this stuff with Jonathon was beginning to get in the way.

The big wide world was pretty busy around that time too. Not least amongst the worldly distractions of paceniks and pop, was a story which hit the headlines with a bang in 1961. This concerned a British double agent called George Blake. He worked for MI6 but had been discovered as simultaneously working for the Russian KGB. It was the stuff of James Bond. The newspapers loved it! He had built up a ring of agents within the British Secret Service and many American secrets had been, as they say in all the best novels, compromised. It was a huge scandal. Blake had been exposed and arrested and his trial was soon to begin. It was a time when Peter, like perhaps thirty million other Britons, avidly bathed in the reams and reams of newsprint all about George Blake, a previously totally unknown man to the public.

Jonathon caught hold of Peter one day, and quite literally hauled him off to their favourite coffee bar in South Ken. He was as white as a sheet and trembling.

'What's the matter?' asked Peter. 'Are you ill or something?'

Jonathon was not usually short on composure. You could always depend on him to string a proper sentence together. Not this time. 'It's him!' he shrieked. Well, whisperingly shrieked would be more accurate.

'Who's him?' asked Peter.

'In the newspaper!' gasped Jonathon.

Peter was no wiser. 'What *are* you talking about?' he demanded

'Blake,' Jonathon managed to get out. 'He's the bloke I've been meeting every week! They'll be after me next!'

This was all far too melodramatic for Peter... until he got the point. Blake hadn't been planning to use Jonathon to expose any communist students he could denounce; he was trying to identify potential communists to ensnare into his spy ring! He was just using Jonathon to find them. It was a marvellous plan. He had established that Jonathon was a sound right-winger so contact with him protected Blake completely while he was out and about seeking his targets. Of course, all this stuff with Jonathon was more by way of a fresh start-up plan; a sort of sideline for Blake. But Peter could see why Jonathon was mightily scared. Nobody wished to get wound into all that sort of stuff.

'You'll be OK,' said Peter, after a while. 'You've been duped but they will be well aware that you're no communist.'

'I bloody well hope so,' moaned Jonathon, 'but they're sure to double check me.'

'Well, maybe that's a good thing,' replied Peter after a few moments' thought. 'That way, you'll end up thoroughly checked and as clean as a whistle.'

An itsy-bitsy trace of colour returned to Jonathon's cheeks, but not too much.

Blake was later found guilty and sent to Wormwood Scrubs prison for forty-two years, possibly the longest prison sentence that had ever been handed down in Britain. Five years later he was sprung by the Russians and magicked out of the country and into Russia, where he still lives, complete with gongs to hang around his treacherous neck. At the time of this tale, all that prison stuff and escaping was ahead of him, however. Jonathon didn't bother with the College Conservative Club any more but buckled down to his chemical engineering degree which he passed well in due course. He became a professional engineer, and in later years, became CEO of an engineering concern in the USA.

Art Club

Peter's social life didn't centre exclusively around Jonathon. One day in the middle of his second year, he met someone new. A bloke called Michael Junor was letting it be known that he was interested in creating an art club for the culture-starved students of Imperial College which, as noted earlier, was a college specialising exclusively in science, engineering and mining. The authorities of the college themselves realised how unbalanced was the educational mix in the place and made great efforts to compensate for this by running Lunchtime Lectures on Tuesdays and Thursdays each week. All students and faculty members were invited to these lectures, given by some extremely interesting and informed people on every kind of topic you might imagine. There was also a kind of Summer School retreat in leafy Surrey, owned by the college, to which small parties could repair for a long weekend's discussion and intellectual binge. But there wasn't an art club. Mike, reading civil engineering, was a dab hand with the oils and loved talking about art and artists. Peter liked the guy from the moment they first met and had some facility with the brushes himself. They found a few other students with similar views so declared an art club formed. They wanted to pursue two activities: to meet every couple of weeks to talk about art, and to set up a life-drawing class. The first was an easy thing to organise. All they had to do was to book one of the small meeting rooms in Beit Hall and turn up.

The second could have been quite difficult but for the fact that next door to Imperial College was the Royal College of Art, with students learning about fine arts, jewellery design, working in glass, industrial design of various kinds, and so on. So one of the founders of the IC art club went round to the Arts College and asked if a drawing life-class could be set up. He couldn't have received a more welcoming and cooperative response; they agreed to arrange everything and even supply a student to teach, or at least, to walk around and make helpful criticism.

All the scientists would be required to do was to pay for the models. A small termly membership fee took care of that and the new culture injection began.

The whole enterprise lasted only one term but the experience was not a waste of time. Peter attended about four life classes but the first was the most memorable. The experience of settling down at an easel with sharpened pencils and of seeing an ample, middle-aged woman remove her thin gown and wriggle into position seared itself into Peter's brain. He had barely seen a naked woman before; certainly not one of his mother's age. He'd seen pictures, of course, mostly pornographic but not, he would hasten to assure you, exclusively. Immediately, he would cite some of the famous nudes of the classicists and impressionists so establishing his *bona fides* within this milieu. This, however, was different. This was REAL and it sure did wobble. The session lasted for an hour before the model smiled at the class and wrapped herself away. Peter had managed to make a passable stab at his nude, he thought, but was far too shy to actually ask the student "teacher" in so many words for his opinion. Even so, he had been given some guidance about line and shade, so he felt that he had learned something. As the embarrassed group of scientists quietly packed up their drawings and pencils, one of them asked the mentor for his overall opinion of this bunch of amateurs.

'Oh, not too bad!' said the young man with much kindness. 'But maybe there shouldn't be so much emphasis on the pubic hair!'

It's true, thought Peter. Some of us avoided drawing the pubes altogether. Others were so determined not to be wimps that we put in far too much effort.

If the life classes could be described as some sort of success, the discussion groups traversed the scale from the sublime to the gor' blimey in three lengthy meetings. At first, there were some almost intelligent meanderings around the ideas of æsthetics which Peter found confusing. It was the last of their gatherings which made the deepest mark. It centred around the question of what constituted a work of art. Peter could not properly recall all the ins and outs of their learned discussion (they were scientists, after all, quite inexperienced in that sort of thing) but he always remembered the last few sallies. One of their number put forward the idea that anything which was deliberately made by conscious effort should be called a "work of art". It was not necessary for the "thing" to be deemed "good" by any æsthetic at all; all that was necessary was that it be deliberately conceived. Deliberation seemed to be the key. As an example, the speaker placed some coins and a keyring on the table before him and announced that that was a work of art. Several of those sitting there began to get a bit restive. Then another speaker came up with the argument to end all arguments; or so it seemed to Peter.

'Suppose,' he said, 'that I walk into an empty room and find these coins and keyring lying around but that I pick them up to inspect them and then toss them back on the table without any thought whatsoever about how they are arranged – a random throw. Is that a work of art if there was no conscious deliberation?'

It seemed the consensus was that it was not.

'Now suppose that I leave the room at that point and someone else comes in, sees the random display, picks up all the items, and then, quite deliberately and carefully, replaces them on the table in exactly the same positions in which he had first seen them. Is *that* a work of art?'

The meeting broke up at that point and someone said, in weary defeat, 'Let's go to the bar and get a beer.'

Æsthetics is clearly a very difficult subject, thought Peter.

That was the end of the Imperial College Art Club, or at least that incarnation of it, but it was not the end of Peter's friendship with Mike.

Posh Digs

Altogether, Peter was lucky enough to stay in Beit Hall, with all its convenience of being right on the central site, for his last two undergraduate years. He performed sufficiently well in his final examinations and in his research year that he was eligible to continue on to work towards a doctorate. Now he really began to enjoy his work again but not to the exclusion of all else that life might have to offer.

His most urgent problem was finding a place to live. He was moaning to Mike about the difficulties of finding somewhere that was both likeable and reasonably close to Imperial. Quite out of the blue, Mike suggested that Peter came to live with him. He was renting what he called a one-room-flat in Sloane Street, an address to make the mouth water. But what on earth was a one-room-flat? Peter went to view the place. It was a front room on the third floor of a five-storey row house in Sloane Street, towards the Sloane Square end. The house was owned by Mr. and Mrs. Rentorne who let out three rooms surplus to their needs. It wasn't clear to Peter, then or later, that they had a financial need to let rooms. The upper floors were accessed *via* a narrow, winding staircase but it, like the more generous stairs between the lower floors, was carpeted and pleasantly decorated. Mike's room, overlooking Sloane Street itself, was in the form of a square and of quite generous proportions. Against two adjacent walls were placed a couple of single sofa beds and there were some comfortable chairs and a tasteful period table and chest of drawers in the room which was itself carpeted wall-to-wall. In comparison with the rooms which Peter had lived in throughout his undergraduate career, this was tasteful and luxurious. The rest of the third floor comprised a smaller, single room, rented by an air stewardess called Isobel, and a small bathroom/toilet shared between the two rooms. On the top floor above was a small self-contained flat rented by another stewardess and her steward boyfriend.

Mike was happy to share his pad with Peter for half the rent, adding that he was likely to be away on many weekends visiting his parents who lived near Bognor Regis. By this time in his life, Peter had acquired a girlfriend and leapt at the possibility of bringing her to his room sometimes when she could get down to London from her work as a teacher in Nottingham, while Mike was away on the south coast. He gratefully accepted Mike's offer and was taken to meet Mrs. Rentorne. Everything was duly arranged, rent was paid and Peter moved in. He lived there for two years altogether and was very happy. It was also a source of many educational experiences – that is, experiences from which he learnt things about life.

There were no proper cooking facilities in their room; just an electric kettle, a toaster and a small electric ring barely big enough to heat a small saucepan. For a long time, Peter and Mike restricted themselves to the kettle and the toaster, using cheap restaurants or the canteen in Beit Hall for their evening meals. From the beginning, they agreed to keep the room tidy as the only way of maintaining a degree of civilisation. That wasn't difficult for they were both naturally tidy young men. After a while, they developed the habit of walking up Sloane Street and into Brompton Road after having eaten the edible but uninspiring food in the canteen at Imperial College, there to indulge in coffee and apple pie with cream in an outlet known as the Kenya Coffee House. The pie portions were generous indeed, the pie centre being some four inches high. The whipped cream served with it covered a delicious four further inches. Mike had begun his career by now and was in a proper job with a proper salary so he could afford such luxuries. Mind you, he had bought a car, an old Lea Francis which was as beautiful as it was expensive to run. Even so, Mike was financially comfortable enough. Peter was still living on a student grant, but by now, a research student's grant. He was, by nature, careful with his money, so that apple pie and cream twice a week was well within his range. Mind you, that was so really only because, unlike so many young lads of his age, he boozed rather little.

That began to change as he got to know Mrs. Rentorne, who with everyone else in the house, he had learned to call by her first name. Rita was wont to sit at a table next to the open door of her L-shaped kitchen on the second floor. Martin, her husband, could be seen in the back room occasionally but was usually out of sight, or in daylight hours, away in a small factory he owned and in which garden gnomes were made, or something like that; Peter never really knew the details. As Rita's tenants climbed the stairs, they were obliged to pass by the open door of her kitchen and it was almost a racing certainty that Rita would be there to accost them and invite them in for a chat. And a glass of Chablis. You could refuse, claiming to be in a frightful hurry, that you were late for a meeting, or whatever came to mind; but truth was that Rita was lonely and everyone felt churlish, to some degree or other, to refuse her hospitality in exchange for a half-hour's chat about the world in general. Sometimes an hour's chat. The Chablis ran out and Rita would press a ten bob note into Peter's hand in a conspiratorial manner, not wanting Martin to see if he was anywhere around, with an instruction to pop across the road into Waitrose, purveyors, amongst much else, of fresh supplies of Chablis. It wasn't too long before Peter realised that he was regaining all of his rent back in kind. He offered to buy a couple of bottles one evening but Rita was adamant. 'Don't be silly. You can't afford that on a student grant. Leave things as they are. Rentorne can afford it!'

Rita's conversation could be rather silly and boring but there was absolutely no doubt that she needed company.

Her children, one of each variety, were about three and six when Peter first joined Mike in Sloane Street. Well that's what Peter guessed with his fathomless depth of parental ignorance. He did fully realise, however, that Rita was not a natural mother, and if Martin was a natural father, it was only to the extent that he paid absolutely no attention to his progeny whatever. So betwixt and between, the kids went to sleep when they became tired, which was usually around nine o'clock in the evening. They slept where they fell, it seemed, for everyone in the house – which really meant the renters in practice – would have to step over the little mites as they ascended and descended the narrow staircase. The kids were bright as buttons in the morning though, so it seemed to Peter that detailed and careful parenting might not be essential.

Growing Up

There's no doubt that Peter was a late developer; as far as sex was concerned, anyway. He was nearly twenty-one before getting his leg over for the first time. He had found a few girlfriends but his clumsy attempts had led nowhere. Truth was that he didn't really know what made girls tick. Now that he had a regular girlfriend, however, with whom he shared life's illicit mysteries, he had calmed down a bit and was becoming somewhat more relaxed in his interactions with the opposite sex. To his surprise, he discovered that he was becoming less unattractive as a result. Even more surprising was his finding that he could achieve some success, not only without trying, but also without desiring it.

This was only too apparent one evening in Sloane Street while sharing a glass or two with Rita. Their ever-wandering area of discussion had moved onto restaurants and Rita began to tell Peter about the *Soup Kitchen* where simple but delicious meals were to be had. In answer to Peter's questioning, she tried to describe its whereabouts. All that Peter was able to comprehend was that it was somewhere not too far from Hyde Park Corner but nicely within the posh area of Belgravia. Rita wouldn't know of any eatery in less salubrious places, thought Peter.

After a few more glasses of Chablis, Peter and Rita were becoming a little silly, perhaps, but decidedly mellow. Rita suddenly suggested that she take Peter to the *Soup Kitchen* for a spot of late supper. Peter wasn't really hungry but was curious to see this much-vaunted establishment so they set off walking there. It wasn't too far really but the cool evening air began to have its effects. In part, it brought about a degree of sobriety but more worrying for Peter was its bringing on a growing feeling of nausea. Rita had taken Peter's arm as they marched on their merry way and Peter's growing awareness of her and of his own long-awaited maturity made him finally comprehend that Rita had designs upon his person. His new-found maturity didn't run, however, to his being able to brush this discovery aside too easily. In short, as their journey progressed, he grew a little fruity.

The restaurant was almost empty when they arrived. It was a cosy place, thought Peter and they settled into a small booth where they could sit closely opposite one another. They began to examine the menu. By this time, the cool evening had well and truly got to Rita. She was beginning to rue her flash of inspiration. 'I'm old enough to be his mother,' she told the waiter who hadn't asked and wasn't interested.

Peter's nausea had, by now, built enormously and was almost as great as his innate sense of decency. He excused himself and carefully but briskly went off to find the restaurant's toilet. He really didn't want to throw up at all but if it had to be, then that was the place. He knew instinctively how to calm his body's reactions to this problem. He had to get cold somehow and stay that way for at least a quarter of an hour. He knew that washing his face with cold water was nowhere near effective enough. So, being the logical little research student that he was, he went into one of the two available cubicles, stripped to his underpants and, as best he could, lay down on the cold terrazzo floor. And there he remained while occasional visitors came in to use the urinal, until he felt well enough to be in complete control of his stomach. Then he got dressed again, inspected himself in the mirror and decided that he had lost his green pallor sufficiently to rejoin society. When he checked his watch, he found that he had absented himself for nearly twenty-five minutes. He walked – somewhat carefully, it must be said – back to the booth where he had left Rita and, without making too much of a fuss, apologised for his long absence.

By this time, Rita had sobered up pretty well completely – certainly enough to realise that she had been making a fool of herself so she suggested that they get a cab immediately and get home to bed; to their separate beds. Peter, without rancour, recognised the wisdom of her words and they went straight back to Sloane Street. All for the best really. Over the following days, both were somewhat embarrassed when they bumped into each other in the house, but equally both were sufficiently polite and sensible that the whole evening soon got more or less forgotten. Thereafter, however, Rita offered, and Peter drank, less of that Chablis.

The house in Sloane Street was no den of iniquity but that wasn't the only such tale to tell. Diana, the stewardess in the flat on the top floor was an absolute blonde bombshell in the eyes of Peter and Mike both. Such a shame that she was spoken for and in love with her bloke. Who were they kidding, for God's sake? She never even noticed them. Someone else who felt the same way about her, though, was Martin Rentorne. Martin was probably about forty-five at that time. He was, Peter thought, a reasonably good-looking fellow and not short of a bob or two, but he had some funny habits. Apart, that is, from being married to Rita and helping to bring up his kids as some kind of stair rats. His most undesirable habit was to sit on the toilet reading his newspaper and leaving the door wide open. Everybody ascending and descending the narrow stairs would, as Mike put it, cop an eyeful of Martin checking the horses. After some months of all this, Mike was not the only one who became convinced that Martin was doing his thing mostly to impress – if that's really the word – the blonde bombshell. Mike mentioned this, as casually as he could one evening, to Diana herself. It brought forth the longest conversation anyone, other than her boyfriend, had ever had with the young lady. Oh yes, she agreed, and added that Martin not only exposed himself, as it were, on the toilet, but at other times, would watch out for her coming down the stairs when he would stand in front of the mirror in the back room and stick out his chest while swaying from side to side. Diana wasn't in the least offended but she did consider the whole thing hilarious and found Martin ridiculous. But she would always smile one of her sweetest smiles at him every time she passed his rooms and occasionally compliment him.

'You *are* looking well today, Martin,' she would say with the most sugar-laden smile.

Rita saw all of this and thought that Diana was a gem.

Sophistication

After a few months in Sloane Street, Peter had suggested that he set up some music in their room. You remember that he had constructed that powerful amplifier as a cheap way to building his own hi-fi set; the one he used for the folk dancing adventures with Mo Mitchell and his wife. It wasn't really deserving of being called hi-fi as he knew full well from his experience of listening to Jonathon's dad's Leak amplifier and the rest when his mind had been blown by *Scheherazade* and *West Side Story*. However, when next Peter went back to see his parents, he returned with the amplifier, turntable, his twelve-inch speaker complete with its nearly three-foot square sound board cut from the old carrying case, and his turntable and record pickup. Mike was astounded by the size of that soundboard and began to question Peter's intentions but Peter had a plan. He had also returned with one or two woodworking tools and he set about cutting the board to fit snugly into the throat of the Victorian fireplace in their room. It was never actually used by them as a fireplace so they lost nothing by all this. Peter's idea was not only to make the speaker blend quietly into the room décor, as it were, but also to use the chimney behind as a huge resonator and so to improve the power and quality of his admittedly poor-quality speaker. It actually worked quite well, and on one occasion, they yanked up the volume to see what the setup could really do. It was quite frightening and far louder than they really needed or wanted so they didn't repeat the experiment but it was nice to know, said Peter, that the thing could really perform when you turned up the wick. Most of the time he and Mike played modern jazz or classical music at decent volume while they enjoyed their occasional home-cooked evening meal or a drink.

Yes, they had graduated to a bit of home cooking! There was little they could do with a single ring and a toaster, particularly when they had agreed not to make the place smell, and even more particularly when neither of them had a clue about cooking. But they could make beans on toast with an egg on top. They heated up a tin of Heinz's baked beans in their only saucepan and put it aside as they poached a couple of eggs in their only frying pan. Easy! The tricky bit came when they had to transfer the slippery eggs onto the beans heaped up onto the pieces of toast. It was tricky because of their dearth of suitable cooking utensils with which to perform that delicate operation. Without a slotted spoon, it seemed that their best option was to use their one and only cooking spoon. It was easy enough to catch the egg from the frying pan of hot water but, as they did not want to swamp their beans on toast with any hot water, the trick was to tilt the spoon, ever so carefully to one side so as to let the slippery poached egg slide off without carrying much of the water with it. To be fair, they became quite adept at this manoeuvre. The trouble was, however, that once the egg had acquired enough momentum to slip off the spoon onto the beans, it then had enough momentum to slip off the beans and onto the floor. Of course, with due care and attention and reapplication with the cooking spoon, said egg could be scooped off the carpeted floor back onto the beans and this time it would stay there because the carpet had absorbed the excess water and no spoon tilting was required. These very practical scientists were thus able to prepare their evening meal. The carpet stain is probably still there.

Now all this evening sophistication was complemented for Peter by the real thing every morning as he walked into college for his day's researching. It was particularly pleasurable for him when the sun was shining. You see, Sloane Street – and just about all streets in central London actually – are filled with houses and mansions without garages; such are the pleasures of inner-city living. So people park their cars outside in the street. However, in Sloane Street and its environs, live many people whose pocket money would match the yearly income of lesser mortals like Peter and Michael, even though the latter now had a "proper" job. Such fortunates don't drive Fords or 2CVs. They drive Rolls-Royces, Bentleys, E-type Jaguars, S-type Mercedes, Maseratis… One must stop drooling; Peter never did. He simply bathed in the glow of these wondrous machines as he walked past first one and then another… and then another. He felt that some of their sophistication rubbed off on him as if he somehow acquired some sliver of ownership as he walked by. It was the same every morning and his avatar's sense of pride only grew. His march into Imperial College took him down Beauchamp Place. Early on, he had learned that this was to be pronounced Beecham Place, just as Cholmondeley is to be pronounced Chumley, or Featherstonhaugh as Fanshaw. How frightfully English! Spot on, he thought. It all seemed much of a piece to Peter: Royces and Jags; Beecham without the pills. He always arrived in the lab in a good humour.

Sad News and Old Friends

After a little more than a year of sharing that posh pad, Mike's father died. Mike had been going down to Bognor quite regularly during the previous few months as his dad had being showing signs of mortality. Peter was left on his own in their Sloane Street flat and suggested to Mike that he pay a larger share of the rent but Mike would have none of it. Some time after the funeral, when family affairs were settled and Mike's mother was calmer, Mike returned to town. But he was soon off again and shortly afterwards, Peter discovered the reason. Mike had found a new girlfriend and he was quite crazy about her. In no time, or so it seemed to Peter, they were married and had found themselves a flat together in South London. Peter and Mike remained friends but inevitably their ways parted.

Now, of course, Peter had to find someone else to share the rent for he could not afford it on his own. As he wandered in to college one morning, he hit on an idea. He knew that Jonathon had found a job in London. Maybe he would like to share? And that's what happened. So Peter was back with his old friend Jonathon. Funny how things work out. They were less close than before, however, partly because Jonathon was busy proving himself in his first job, naturally enough, but also because he too had found himself a young lady who was, in time, to become his wife. In any case, Peter too was getting ever more preoccupied with his research and with the girl he was to marry in a little over two years. So, all in all, the pad in Sloane Street was not always filled and life took on a quieter style.

Sometimes it was a little too quiet for Peter and he was happy to develop a friendship he and Michael had begun earlier with the stewardess who lived in the back room on their floor. Isobel was a friendly, attractive, dark-haired girl who was frequently away from her flat in far-flung destinations of world travel as part of her job on international routes. She was madly in love with a pilot with whom she regularly flew. Trouble was, he was married. Peter had never come across anyone in these circumstances before, and with his ever-ready curiosity, wanted to know all the ins and outs. Isobel was only too happy to tell all for she was as frustrated as hell whenever she and her lover were back in town, him with his wife and she all alone. On one occasion, Peter was naive and stupid enough to agree to call up the boyfriend on the phone, the idea being to hand over the instrument to Isobel when he came on. As he was led to expect, the boyfriend's wife answered the phone and when asked, Peter said he was a friend of John's (or whatever his name was). Things did not go according to plan, however, for the lady immediately sensed that Peter was no friend of her husband but was phoning on behalf of the girlfriend (Peter hadn't thought that the wife might know; he really was very gauche) and she gave him a very strongly worded piece of her mind. Peter dropped the phone like a hot potato and resolved never to get into anybody's business like that ever again. A good, if hard, lesson.

He remained friendly with Isobel, however, and would join her in her room occasionally for a late-evening game of canasta. Jonathon caught them together like that once, dressed in their pyjamas and dressing gowns, sipping wine and flipping cards. It really was completely innocent but Jonathon needed some persuading. Peter simply couldn't see why two grown adults shouldn't enjoy an innocent evening together like that. He had certainly grown more relaxed with women as the years had passed but maybe had yet to learn something more about self-protection! That was certainly the case when, on another evening some while later, Rita opened Isobel's door on them to see the pair of them at it; Peter with his pipe blowing smoke, he and Isobel supping from glasses of wine, each with a hand of cards. Rita's face was quite thunderous; she had clearly been told of goings on in her house. She said nothing, however, and left the room. Peter felt he had to explain the circumstances to her the following morning so that there were no misunderstandings. He came away from the conversation unconvinced of any success but a little wiser.

You know, that was probably more or less the end of Peter's informal education as a bachelor. He was married fairly soon after these events and moved away to live in Chiswick. His work progressed well and his life became extraordinarily busy.

At eighty, he knows only too well how little he really knows.

DOWN TO EARTH

I had known Denis well – but his wife, Marion, only peripherally – through work some years earlier. Denis had been my boss or, at least, one of them. He had a delightfully light touch in that capacity. It was during those days that Denis was knighted and so I ought to have introduced them as Sir Denis and Lady Felton, I suppose. While I have absolutely no doubt that Denis, at least, was delighted by the honour, in dealings with almost everybody, they separately and collectively preferred the handle dropped. Marion felt particularly strongly about this, even more so after Denis' ridiculously premature death from pancreatic cancer in his early sixties.

'Just call me Marion,' she insisted whenever anyone used her title. 'I really can't stand all that formality, you know.' Actually, she didn't say that. She said that she couldn't stand all that "crap". I had preferred not to say that lest you think Marion was coarse and uneducated. She was neither. It's just that she really felt strongly about the issue.

You might think that she put on this dismissive show in false humility, but I insist not for as Red and I got to know her more and more, we knew it to be utterly genuine. Forgive me; I should have introduced myself. My name is Sam. My wife's is Red; well it's not really but we have called her that for as long as I have known her in honour of her beautiful, flowing, wavy red hair. It's perfectly possible, you know, to fall in love with hair like that. She couldn't reciprocate, mind you; I'm as bald as a coot.

Denis and Marion lived in grand official accommodation in town but had bought a small cottage in a neighbouring village as a private escape and with a view to its being their retirement home much later. As I intimated, that retirement came inexpressively sadly far too soon. I still retain many happy memories of Denis's urbanity and sensitivity – above all, of his wicked sense of humour. He could laugh at himself as much as at anyone else. He hated pomposity, but like any other down-to-earth human being, could fall right into a pompous trap of his own making.

I remember laughingly telling him once about the art of lecturing being "The casting of imitation pearls before real swine", a sentiment which had tickled me from the moment I'd first heard it.

Denis was amused but couldn't resist the opportunity of cutting me down to size. 'Never forget,' he intoned, 'that a lecturer is in a position of privilege and must show his audience due respect at all times.'

Denis's eyes would twinkle when he said something provocative or just downright funny. You know, thinking about that; his eyes defined him. The life radiating from his face and the twinkle in his eyes said far more than any tongue pushed into a cheek could ever do. I rose to the challenge.

'Now I've been patronised by an expert!' I exclaimed. You could say things like that to Sir Denis. He just loved it.

'Bugger off!' he replied and his eyes twinkled the more.

'I suppose that's an example of *droit du seigneur,*' I replied.

'Too right!' he said with some force. You couldn't argue with that.

Well, it was some time later that Red and I bought a cottage in the same village, although we hadn't been aware of the coincidence at the time. Denis had been dead some five years or so. Marion had settled into their retirement cottage, and being the steely woman she was, had found a new life and new energy there. She was financially more than secure and their son, Robin, by now in his thirties, popped in to see her every week, more or less, often with his partner, Zoe, and daughter, Jacki. Marion was a gregarious soul, thank God, and had more friends than you could point a stick at. Denis had been a distinguished scientist and nobody's fool. Marion, however, more than held her own. Her strength lay, not in science, but in fine art. She was a thoroughly successful amateur artist, specialising in pen drawing and aquatint, amongst other techniques. Most of her work sold quickly, and indeed, Red and I commissioned an etching of our cottage. We still have it. And, like Denis himself, she was also a more-than-competent gardener so Red and I begged cuttings from her as we set up our own place. We hadn't expected to find Marion in that village but it happened that way; we were so lucky. So it was there that we got to know her well and we would visit each other's homes for dinner every so often. We lived only a few hundred yards apart.

Hers was a delightful cottage It exuded homeliness, comfort and taste. I mean the taste of an artist. The walls were covered with paintings and drawings, many by Marion herself, arranged in a seemingly random way. One, by her son Robin, an oil of eggs frying in a pan, had been composed with such mastery that I, for one, could never take my eyes off it. I guess that, in some way, Robin had managed to throw the pan forward out of the canvas, in the manner rather of Van Gogh's painting of his bed. In that case, the technique is clear; the master had drawn two different perspectives for the bed and the floor on which it stood. How this amateur had achieved his visual shock, I never worked out.

Marion's kitchen was a total mess. Well, to fussy smarts like Red and me it was. There was a carefree collection of cupboards, many without doors, barely supporting a bright red worktop in several sections and at differing heights. Pans and various cooking gadgets hung from butchers' hooks above a small, centrally-placed table with a scrubbed pine top. You had to be careful if you sat down there for a cup of tea. Another of Marion's many talents was making chutneys and jams. One part of her worktop was more or less covered with a jumble of jars, some Kilner, some covered with greaseproof paper held on with elastic bands. Every jar was labelled in her beautiful artist's script. Her cooker was at a low level, old-fashioned with four gas burners on top, suitably adapted to bottled gas for there was no town gas laid on in the village. It was barely more modern than the one my mother had used for years, years ago. No matter – Marion prepared some delicious stews and roasts from this unfashionable equipment. One could not but admire her – and Denis's – ability to cut to the quick. They did what worked. For them.

I never saw Denis looking smart. Even on formal occasions, his bow tie was invariably crooked, his dinner suit slightly crumpled and his hair looked as if his comb had broken midway through its duties. At other times, he wore a checked shirt with its collar askew, trousers whose creases had disappeared years ago, and a jacket with pockets even more full of junk than mine. We were both pipe smokers in those days so I could well imagine what he was carrying. I have to admit that it has always been a mystery to me how some pipe smokers are able to maintain a modicum of dress dignity. If Denis's garb had a homely, comfortable look about it, his slightly fleshy facial features had no less of a lived-in look. Again, it was all fit for purpose.

Marion, too, put comfort and common sense above all else. Her hair was plentiful and kind of neat enough but no more than that. Her dress sense lacked finesse, shall I say. She was not dowdy though, for she occasionally wore some quite bright colours, but one got the impression that her selection for the day had been made in haste or while distracted, or maybe at random. In all this, she was pretty well at one with her husband. Where she differed, perhaps, was in facial features. In fairness, women are supposed to be the fair sex, to have their unfair bonus of beauty. And, also in fairness, we mustn't forget the magical twinkle in Denis's eye. But Marion's face was – quite simply – beautiful. Not classically so as might have blessed a film star but deeply, meaningfully, significantly so. And that derived as much as anything from the intelligence of her expressions, the kindness of her glances. She had no real need of elegant dresses. She was complete as she came. Like Denis, Marion Felton was at home in her skin.

As I explained, she was widowed by the time that Red and I came to know her well, and from time to time, she would fly off to distant shores to stay with old friends or to explore new parts of the world. Like anyone else, she often suffered jet lag on her return, but unlike others, she met its challenges with an honesty and freedom I'd never seen before. When she felt tired, she went to bed and slept. When she woke up, she got up and read or made a meal or painted a picture, no matter what time of the day or night. "It will sort itself out in due course" was her mantra. It did.

In our early days in that village, Red and I were pretty strapped for cash. I had my academic job and research which were pretty much full-time and any spare time I could make was filled with gardening and building or altering our home. Red's job was full time but finished after the required hours. Nevertheless, she ran our home, feeding me, our cats and the more or less endless stream of visitors we both loved having in our cottage. Even so, she found time to join in village enterprises, acting as unpaid secretary to the parochial church council for some thirteen years and helping organise both the annual church fete and the village show as well. God knows how many cakes she baked over the years to help raise money for re-leading the church roof. Other than in heaven, her reward was to meet and get to know nearly everybody in the village. I reaped the benefit of that. Nevertheless, none of these activities brought in money; indeed, the opposite, really, for we paid for all the ingredients in those damn cakes! Somehow, Red found time to make a few bob by painting neighbours' cottage window frames. When Marion got to hear about that, she formed a tactful plan to help us out without being patronising in any way. She asked Red to paint the outside of her cottage. Marion herself had very wonky legs, and later, a hip replacement which went a bit wrong so she was in no fit state to climb ladders. She offered Red a generous amount of money to do the job for her and we were very grateful. Why did I not do the job? You might well ask. Well, let me tell you I am an out-and-out coward when it comes to ladders. I am terrified of heights except when wrapped in the metal tube of an aeroplane fuselage. I did help Red in one small way. I stood on the bottom rung of the ladder as safety weight while she climbed towards heaven with her paint pot. At first, I made the mistake of looking up at her as she climbed but my imaginings of her climb made me feel sick immediately. From then on, I kept my gaze firmly fixed on the garden around us. So Red did the job. Afterwards, she did confess to being more than a little nervous up that very long ladder but she did the job and earned us a welcome contribution to our household exchequer. Marion's generosity was as subtle as it was welcome.

I explained that we came to meet so many other villagers through Red's endeavours in the church. One couple, however, we came to know through Marion herself. Indeed, they were immediate neighbours. They spent half their time in London and half in their cottage in the country. Jill was a quite famous opera and recital singer while her partner's career centred round the historical and literary side of opera together with his writing a long and learned study of Wagner. We spent many happy hours with Patrick and Jill, who provided a mixture of high art, intelligence, urbanity and very occasionally, childlike simplicity. Towards the end of our life in that village, Jill was offered the chance to take the lead in a brand-new opera about the Duchess of Argyll called "Powder her Face". The duchess had reputedly been a highly-sexed lady whose marriage ended in a scandalous divorce in 1963 involving nearly salacious pictures of a "headless" man. The opera included a scene with a musical depiction of fellatio. Like all our friends who came to hear about this, Red and I cracked up about the whole enterprise. Patrick leant over our garden fence one afternoon and breathlessly informed us of the essence of Jill's new role.

'Jill has to pretend to perform fellatio on stage!' he told us conspiratorially with gales of laughter from us all: Jill, Patrick, Red and me.

A couple of days later, Marion also told us all about the story. We explained that we'd already heard it from the horse's mouth. Perhaps that's an unhappy phrase but I'll leave it in.

Marion continued, 'I didn't know what fellatio was… '

We found her confession astonishing, remembering how intelligent and well-read she was.

'… So I asked my son, Robin.'

This tale was becoming more hilarious by the second.

'He said, "Oh Mother! It's oral sex". Oh! Is that all? I replied. I just hadn't heard the word before.'

The deed, yes – the word, no. Marion could be so honest – so utterly outrageous.

Marion could also be very determined. She once told Red about Denis coming home after some conference or other in September of that year, blowing hard, angry with the world, it seemed.

'I've had it with Christmas,' he said. 'It's only September and everywhere you go they're playing "Jingle Bells" and all that rubbish. Christmas is months away. It's all rubbish! We won't be celebrating Christmas this year. Do you hear?'

'Yes, dear,' replied Marion meekly.

For God's sake, they had been married long enough. Denis should have understood what Marion's meekness might bring forth. For a clever man, he could be so slow. When Christmas came there were no signs of it in the Felton household. No Christmas decorations, no tree, no special lights. On Christmas Day itself, there were no smells of cooking either. Denis wandered into the kitchen and opened the oven door. Nothing there. He opened the cupboard door wherein lay the large tin which normally contained mince pies at Christmas. Empty.

'Where's the turkey? Where are my mince pies? I can't find any signs of Christmas pudding.' He was becoming quite agitated, even angry.

Marion smiled sweetly at him and reminded him of his edict more than three months earlier. 'You said Christmas was not to be celebrated this year. You were adamant. So there is no turkey, nor mince pies, nor Christmas pudding. You are welcome to join me in a ham sandwich.'

'You know, Red,' she told my wife, 'he turned quite purple for a moment, almost puce!'

'Shall we go out?' continued Marion as Denis tried to control himself.

'We stayed in with a sandwich in the end,' Marion told Red who was collapsing in a heap beside her. It's amazing what you normally don't get to know about people.

It was during one of our evening visits to dine with Marion when I noticed a small, framed photograph perched amongst many others on top of one of her side-tables. It wasn't a well-composed or arty photograph at all. Quite the reverse. It showed a somewhat younger Denis than I remembered, dressed in baggy trousers and over-sized jumper and standing in front of a large pram. I presumed that the baby carriage was for their granddaughter, Jacki, although she wasn't evident in the picture. I supposed that she was crouched or laid down and hidden from view. As we began our evening with hearty gins and tonic (Marion was rather partial to her G&Ts), I began working out when that photo must have been taken. I guessed that Denis had been in his mid-fifties. So Robin would have been in his mid-twenties and Jacki two years old, perhaps. Yes, that would be right.

'Whoever took that snapshot should have waited for Jacki to pop up again,' I remarked. It took a second or two for Marion to understand what I was getting at.

'Not everything in this world is as it first seems,' she replied enigmatically.

I waited for her to elaborate but she dashed off to attend to something in the kitchen and by the time she returned, the moment had passed. Over dinner, we chatted about all sorts of things, none of which I remember now but I would guess related to both national and local news of the times as well as anecdotes about people in the village. That was how we passed so many a bucolic evening in those days. I can't remember quite how we got onto it but the subject of dogs came up. Red and I were – and still are – cat people. We like dogs but we get cats. Marion had one of each at the time we knew her. Her cat, Oliver, was a somewhat large – I would say, overfed – lump of black fur who had a rather grumpy personality. We had a pair of Burmese cats who wore their hearts on their sleeves and poured out love like the Trevi fountains of Rome. Oliver seemed not to like visitors of any kind even though we tried ever so hard to be agreeable and we firmly believed that we were God's gift to felines. Marion's dog, on the other hand, a dachshund-kind of make, as I was wont to say, though somewhat long in the tooth, was a friendly enough chap, accepting strokes and tickles from any source at all. I spoke of my approval of small dogs around the house.

'Altogether less work, less food and more room for us,' I pontificated. The conversation wandered off into breeds we especially admired. I spoke about what I considered to be the poshest of dogs, namely the Afghan hound. 'So elegant,' I suggested.

'We had one of those,' replied Marion to my total amazement. She and Denis were not the sort of people, I thought, to own an Afghan hound. She caught the look on my face. 'I know,' she said. 'Not the sort of dog peasants like us would have.' Hardly peasants, but she was right. 'Entirely Denis's idea. To this day, I have absolutely no idea why he wanted one. We called him Clarence. Sometimes Denis would put on a posh accent and call him Clarence from Chorley. So Denis, himself, fully understood the super-posh breed he had chosen. I do admit that Clarence was an exquisite animal. So beautiful. Taller than your waist-height, long flowing hair that only some female starlet should wear, a long and very thin nose. I was going to say "snout" but Clarence would have been mortified by such a description. Oh, yes! He was elegance personified, or should that be canisified? Sorry, my Latin always left something to be desired. But let me tell you: that dog was the stupidest animal in the whole wide world. Beautiful but no brains whatsoever!'

Some diatribe, I thought. 'Trouble with dogs,' I offered, 'is that you have to take them for walks. Even if you like walking, it may not be at a time convenient to you.'

'And the dog may not know whether he wants to walk or not,' rejoined Marion. I asked her what she meant by that.

'Well, Clarence would ask Denis to take him out for a walk. Usually around five o'clock in the afternoon. He made quite a fuss if Denis prevaricated. The dog always won and off they would go together, striding out with Clarence's mane blowing in the breeze and his head erect. An hour or so later, Denis would return, carrying Clarence in his arms. Denis was puffing fit to bust. After all, Clarence was a big boy. Denis would explain that they got as far as the mill down Reynold's Lane, which is about a mile and a half I would guess, before Clarence would sniff around a bit and then lie down in the long grass. Denis would let him be for a moment or two before urging him back onto his feet. "Come on now, Clarence. Time to go back home". Clarence would not move. "C'mon Chorley; home time". Clarence would not move. Denis told me that he would use distinctly Anglo-Saxon epithets eventually, but Clarence would not move. As I told you, Clarence was a very stupid dog. Denis had no option but to carry the silly animal home.'

'So who was taking whom for the walk?' I asked.

'Exactly,' replied Marion, clearly reliving the whole scene. 'Anyway,' she continued, 'after two more "walkies" of that kind, Denis swore not to take him out again. "He's *your* dog", I insisted. Well it so happens that it was the time of the church fete and Denis had popped his head in to show solidarity and all that. He returned with a large pram. That pram you noticed in the photograph before dinner, Sam. Denis was nothing if not an empiricist, a lateral thinker you might say. Next day, he took the dog for his walk but pushed the pram along with him. When Clarence put on his act and refused to get up and walk home, Denis picked him up, plonked him in the pram and pushed him home like a baby. It all became quite a habit, really. If anyone stopped and asked what was afoot, Denis would explain that Clarence had been hurt in a road accident or something and that he was just giving him the chance of some air.'

'I'm not too sure that Clarence really was stupid, you know,' I said.

'Oh! Did I say Clarence?' replied Marion.

Red and I collapsed in hysterics. We did so love that couple. So down to earth. Both gone from us now, I'm afraid.

A LIKELY STORY

Playing the Numbers

I checked my Lotto numbers in the little machine at the front of the counter in the newsagent's and it came up with the oh-so-familiar response, "Not a winning ticket. Better luck next time".

'That's amazing!' I said to the proprietor of my regular haunt. 'Three times in a row! How likely is that?' I didn't expect any reply and I didn't get one. Geoff and I have an understanding. 'I shall take my custom elsewhere,' I continued.

Stony-faced, he stood there with a slight tremble. 'Heart-broken,' he replied.

I'd like you to understand this business of doing the lottery. It's a numbers-plus sort of occupation. Let me explain; although, I must apologise to those whose mantra is "I don't do numbers", but look: at least half of life is numbers; get used to it. Here we go.

The Lotto game offers forty-nine numbers. Straight away, you might ask, "Why forty-nine instead of fifty, surely an æsthetically more pleasing number – more rounded, shall we say". Well, I would guess it's partly because forty-nine equals seven times seven so that they can print an alluring array of seven number boxes in each of seven rows. Patronising buggers. The second reason is surely to do with reducing your chances of winning. Let's look at those chances for a moment. You are to put crosses on six of the forty-nine numbers. For your first choice, there are forty-nine ways of doing that. Obviously, 'cos you can put your cross in box number one or box two or three… all the way to box forty-nine. For your next cross, you have only forty-eight choices because you have filled in one already and you can't put two crosses into the same box. For the third, you have forty-seven empty boxes to choose from; and so it goes. Well, they ask you to choose six numbers altogether so that the number of ways in which you can do that is 49 x 48 x 47 x 46 x 45 x 44. Using reams of paper and a pencil, or since you have far more sense, by employing the calculator on your mobile phone, you can work out that multiplication to get 10,068,347,520. So, you might think, there are over ten billion – ten thousand million – ways of choosing your six numbers! Your chance of choosing the correct numbers is one in over ten billion. What on earth is the point of coughing up your dosh

Ah! But things are not that bleak. That's because the little calculation we just made assumed that the order in which we have to choose the winning numbers is important – that the first number we chose had to agree with the first number the lottery machine chose – that the second number we chose had to agree with the second chosen by the machine, and so on. But that ain't so. The lottery people aren't that cruel. The order doesn't matter, just the winning numbers. So we have to be a mite cleverer to work out the odds of that. We need to know how many ways there are of choosing those same six winning numbers. That's the same as if we had those six numbers marked on billiard balls, for example, and we put those balls into six little boxes. How many ways can that be done? Well we can put the first of the six balls into any one of the six boxes in six ways, the second ball into any one of the remaining five boxes and so on; so that the total number of ways is 6 x 5 x 4 x 3 x 2 x 1, which is 720. In other words, there are seven hundred and twenty ways of choosing the *same* six numbers. Altogether then, our chance of winning the lottery is one in 10,068,347,520 ÷ 720, which as any five-year-old knows is 13,983,816; that is just under fourteen million to one. That's much better than ten billion to one, isn't it? So off you go and spend your quid. If you're a miserable sod, you might still argue that fourteen million to one are still lousy odds and hang onto your hard-earned cash. Well yes! Of course. That way you'll be a dollar better off. But if you were to win, despite those odds, you might be one million poundsbetter off! Therein lies the lure, of course.

And here's another way of looking at all this. If you don't buy a ticket, your chances of winning are zero, or infinity to one against. If you do buy a ticket, your chances are, as we've seen, about fourteen million to one against. So your chances of great enrichment by buying a ticket have improved by infinity divided by 14 million, roughly. So you're infinitely better off! Yes, yes! Alright – a nineteenth century, German mathematician named Georg Cantor might have had something to say about that argument – but he's dead. And even if you are unhappy with my reasoning, consider this. Lightning doesn't strike randomly. You tend to get flares in groups. They cluster. Referring to our game of Lotto, any six numbers are as likely to be selected by the Lotto machine as any other, aren't they? Well, only *in the long run*. If we play the game for ever, the selection 1, 2, 3, 4, 5 and 6 is just as likely to win as 42, 5, 17, 26, 31 and 7. So why not just select 1, 2, 3, 4, 5 and 6 every week? That's easier to remember. But you can't bring yourself to do that, can you? Why not? Two reasons really, which are actually one and the same. In the long run, we're all dead anyway; and, in the short run, the Lotto machine will select numbers which cluster together in funny ways rather than being totally random. A lot of mathematics has been done on this clustering question but I'd hazard the guess that, like me, you have no stomach for it.

So there you go; there you have it, as the prince said in *Amadeus*, there it is. You pays your money and takes your chance. So, I ask, why the hell hasn't it been my turn yet? I've tried hard. I've done my bit; now you do yours! At this point, my bond with the rest of humanity is complete. I don't quite know how likely I am to win the lottery but knowing something about the theory of probability does not help my chances.

Alright; you have been very patient with all this mathematical stuff and I thank you. My name is Daniel Mallow, by the way, a very good friend of Patrick Morgan, whom I must now introduce to you.

A Caring Man

Pat Morgan, like me, is entering his early fifties. He has had his moments but the fact is he's never married. He likes women and they seem to like him well enough, but no permanent relationship has come his way. He admits that he does feel lonely occasionally, but truth to tell, so do some married people. Most of the time, Pat is perfectly content, enjoying encounters with all sorts of people as they occur. He insists that he is generally content, happy in his skin, and as fulfilled as the next, financially secure, person.

Pat is a chartered accountant. He knows full well that some people imagine such an occupation to be rather boring but that's because they don't understand the subject, and rather obviously, don't like numbers; even more, they have little taste for order. Patrick operates on a freelance basis. To some extent, this is a precarious existence in that his contracts can dry up occasionally and he will be left to live off his savings for a while. But he is very good at his job and never has to wait too long before some institution or business calls upon his skills. He has become well known in the game over the years, so work seeks him out rather than the reverse. Take the job he's just finished, for example. The Catholic Church had asked him to examine the finances of one of their schools. The school bursar and his assistants had prepared accounts each year, as required, but last year, profits were markedly down in comparison with the year, even the decade, before. Pat's brief was to check the whole of the school's business to make sure that all was above board – or, as was clearly intimated to him, that the bursar was honest. Patrick knows his way round balance sheets, and in no time, it was abundantly clear to him how the school managed its financial affairs. Put at its simplest, it was too damn honest. The school had decided to build a new laboratory block and to pay for it out of the continuing profits it made from educating its pupils. Nothing could have been simpler except that it tried to do all this within a ridiculously short time. Essentially, it mortgaged against the current and next four years' income instead of spreading the load over a much longer time frame, including setting aside some of the earlier years' profits in anticipation of the build. Had it done that, the bottom line would have been pretty smooth, year on year, certainly smooth enough not to arouse the suspicions of the Church hierarchy. The school is tremendously successful. While providing an adequate education to its pupils, it did what the Church has always done best, namely, make pots of money. Had the bursar set up various contingency funds into which he deposited modest sums each year, he would have built up a nice piggy bank to raid when the time came to splurge. But he hadn't. He had preferred to tackle the build up-front, as it were, and forward a significantly smaller profit to headquarters than in the immediately preceding years. A little smoothing would have been far more tactful. You could say that the bursar was just too naive. In the end, it fell to Patrick to word his report so as to put the bursar in the best possible light while making his probity abundantly clear. In a separate report to the man himself, he gave some pointers to a less astringent style of management for the future. It had all been a simple job for Patrick. It had paid well and was over and done with in short order. He likes jobs like that for, not only can he complete his task quickly, nobody gets hurt. Not all audits are so pleasant nor so simple but Patrick spends whatever time is necessary to get it right. He gives value for money but his services can be quite costly in the end. No more so than when he is called upon to advise on the restructuring of some company or other. This really does involve a great deal of homework – about the company products, raw materials, the market and so on. Invariably he begins from scratch, having virtually no knowledge of the business. But it is that ignorance coupled with high intelligence, the fresh eye of an open mind, which leads him through the morass. He enjoys it all. He loves the forensic probing into reams of documents to get at the truth and the truth is never as complicated as the tricks people play to cover up their misdeeds. Whenever Patrick sees a break in the clouds of obfuscation, he knows he is nearly home. He always enjoys that breakthrough, that relief, that release of all tension and the certitude that comes with it. He enjoys studying back-stories. So much so that he spends much of his free time reading books and magazines in pursuit of his hobbies. Occasionally, he has joined clubs or attended meetings to further his knowledge. It was in one such meeting that he first met Elisabeth. But I'm getting ahead of myself. Sorry.

Make Like an Egyptian

You see, a long time ago – actually when still a boy – Patrick became fascinated by the bird-men to be found, for example, in Ancient Egyptian hieroglyphs. You've probably come across pictures of them yourself – creatures with the body of a man and the head of a bird; as often as not, a falcon. They're undoubtedly striking, and I for one find them to be somewhat solid, believable images. That, of course, might just be a comment on the draughtsmanship of – or carving skill in – these glyphs. Maybe, maybe not, but over the years, Patrick has almost developed a fetish for these mythical beings. He has read dozens of books and articles about them and learned, amongst other things, that one of the most important deities of ancient Egypt was a bird-man called Horus. He had other names, too. Different forms of Horus have been depicted in stone, ivory or gold, for example, at different times in history and Egyptologists have had a merry old time collating, sieving, imagining and asserting. If you think I'm going to spend our time together summarising all their professional constructs, you've got another think coming. That doesn't mean that there's no interest to be found in that field. Pat certainly found it fascinating and, if you'll bear with me, I'll hazard to suggest that you will do so also. But you'll have to make do with a précis, I'm afraid. Just understand, please, that Patrick has boned up on, if not all, then a huge tranche of the vast literature of this field. Try this as a taster.

The earliest recorded mention of Horus was as the first national god specifically related to a ruling pharaoh. Eventually, the pharaoh came to be regarded as a manifestation of Horus in life and of Osiris, his dad, in death. Horus is often found described as the son of Isis and Osiris and he plays a pivotal role in the so-called Osiris myth where he is shown as Osiris's heir and a rival to his uncle, Set, the murderer of Osiris. Elsewhere, Hathor is said to be his mother but sometimes, his wife.

OK – got all that? No? Well, let me fill you in a little. Some of the oldest texts, called the Pyramid Texts, were inscribed on the wall of a subterranean room in one of the ancient pyramids. They date from the period 2400 to 2300 BC. It is there that the idea of the pharaoh being Horus in life and Osiris in death seems to originate. In death, Osiris was united with the other gods; and new incarnations of Horus succeeded the dead pharaoh on earth as a new pharaoh. It is quite likely that this lineage was used to explain and justify pharaonic power. It would seem that little we are familiar with in modern politics is new. The gods represented all cosmic and terrestrial forces in ancient Egypt so that identification of Horus with both gods and pharaohs in this way provided the justification for pharaohs having dominion over *all* the world. You have to admire the bare-faced, jaw-dropping cheek of those pharaohs, don't you? By the way, all this stuff about Horus seemed to have been discarded some centuries later by the identification of the pharaohs with Ra, the sun-god. Seems Horus was given the bird. However, that is not our concern because it wasn't Pat's concern. This yarn is complicated enough without wandering off into byways. So back we go.

Horus, it seems, was born to the goddess Isis after she gathered all the dismembered body parts of her murdered husband Osiris. All, that is, apart from his penis which was thrown into the Nile where it was eaten by catfish – or a crab, depending upon your sources – and their preferences, I presume. Isis used her magical powers to resurrect Osiris from his parts and to construct a new phallus in order to conceive her son. In case you're enjoying this too much, I must tell you that older accounts report the penis as surviving. Regardless of this spoiler, Isis fled the Nile Delta marshlands to hide from her brother, Set, who had killed Osiris earlier in a jealous rage and was fearfully but confidently expected to kill her son also. Isis escaped, however, and bore her divine son, Horus. So what was all that stuff about the penis all about? It seems that the ancient Egyptians were as fascinated by phalluses and sex as Patrick is by bird-men. Read on.

I mentioned earlier that this story appears to have originated in those early Pyramid Texts. It might be better to say that they appear to be the earliest *record* because goodness knows how much further back the story began in an oral form. Perhaps it began as someone's dream, someone who had the gift of the gab and carried many followers with him, or her. I don't know, but of course neither does anyone else because for us, learning the ropes some thousands of years later, there are only the glyphs. By remarkable scholarship, those glyphs have been translated – if that's the correct word for reading pictures – but we must always remember that the translators, however learned they were, inevitably put their own gloss upon the basic yarn. It seems that those ancient Egyptians had, by the time of the carving of the glyphs, constructed a somewhat tight political framework within which the old myths could operate. I won't go into this too deeply but let me give just a flavour of it all.

Isis told her son, Horus, to protect the Egyptian population from uncle Set, the god of the desert and murderer of Horus's father Osiris. Horus battled with Set frequently, in part to avenge his father, but also to choose the rightful ruler of Egypt – eye on the main chance, you might say. In due course, Horus came to be associated with Lower Egypt and he became its patron. Now, in one story, Set is shown trying to demonstrate his dominance by seducing Horus and by having sexual intercourse with him. You see, dominance *via* sex is nothing new. Horus, however, puts his hand between his thighs to catch Set's semen and then throws it into the river so that nobody may say that he had been inseminated by Set. Horus then spreads his own semen on a lettuce leaf. Lettuce was uncle Set's favourite food, by the way, but he didn't notice the salad cream, apparently. Horus and Set then visited the gods in order to settle the argument as to who should rule over Egypt. Who had dominated whom? The gods listened first to Set's claim of dominance. They called his semen forth but it answered from the river, thus invalidating his claim. When Horus said *he* had dominated Set, the gods called forth *his* semen which answered, of course, from inside Set; game, set and match, you might say. But the nerve of the man! Set still refused to accept the judgement and many of the gods were getting more than a little weary of eighty or so years of fighting over this. So Horus and Set challenged each other to a boat race in which each boat was made of stone. You can see why Pat became so fascinated with all this, can't you? Cunning old Horus; *his* boat wasn't *actually* made of stone but rather wood, painted to resemble stone. No, silly. Eh? Set's boat sank, of course, so that Horus won the race, and the throne of Egypt. It seems that Set was awarded a consolation prize, however. He was named as lord of the desert and its oases. Too bad oil hadn't been found in those days.

To cut this long story a little shorter, let me just say that compromises were reached in due course, and as I mentioned above, Horus the bird-man was replaced eventually by Ra, the sun-god. Ra, ra, ra! Alright, I know it isn't fair to rubbish all the painstaking scholarship of generations of Egyptologists. In fact it's cheap, but we have to get where we're going within a reasonable space. In any case, I'm not picking on the Egyptologists but rather on the antics of the ruling class of ancient Egypt. This, indeed, was how my friend, Patrick, came to see all this. Because before all this conjectured – and maybe true – political manoeuvring of long-held, and presumably revered, beliefs, we seem to have lost the original point; namely, why was a bird-man conceived in the first place? Was this idea unique? Patrick put this question to Elisabeth repeatedly. Yes, alright then; it's time I introduced this lady into our story for she begins to assume an ever-greater importance to us and Patrick both.

Soul Mates

It was at a lecture at one of Patrick's hobby meetings when he first clapped eyes on a young lady who was to become such an important part of his lives. Don't change that Ms. Editor. She was much younger than Pat, in her mid-twenties he guessed, neatly dressed in a rather precise kind of way. She was no classic beauty but Pat was immediately attracted to her delicate features, her fine nose and especially her sparkling eyes which advertised a clear and insightful intelligence. She had asked a question of the speaker at that meeting but Pat couldn't remember what it was now. What he did remember, however, was how struck he had immediately been by her clear diction, and above all, by the gentleness of her manner. All of this was reinforced later when they exchanged names over tea and buns after the lecture. Their initial exchange was, quite naturally, about whether they each came regularly to meetings like this. I suppose it was a somewhat genteel version of "Do you come here often", but you have to start somewhere, don't you? As it happens, it was the first lecture on ancient Egypt for both of them so their meeting was fortuitous. Unlikely, maybe. Perhaps. Anyway, Patrick chanced his arm and suggested that she might care to join him for a proper drink in one of his favourite pubs not too far away. He liked the place because it was quiet and you could hear yourself think and your companions talk. It seemed that Elisabeth was also in an arm-chancing mood that day and so began a great adventure for them both.

They quickly discovered that neither was encumbered with a spouse or similar; neither had been married; neither had children. Neither was rich but each was sufficiently comfortable financially to be independent of anybody else. Elisabeth was a freelance illustrator, mostly for those requiring technical drawings in what might be classed broadly as the biological area. She mentioned that her most recent drawings had been of rare birds. Was it just fortuitous that she had chosen to mention that particular topic? It got straight to Patrick, though, who had always had a passion for birds. Not that he was a twitcher, he hastened to assure her. She had asked what was the matter with twitchers but he assured her that there was nothing the matter with them; it was just that he wasn't one of them. He just liked birds. He liked watching them but had no intention of spending hours in boxes with binoculars. At home, he fed birds regularly and enjoyed their company. He generally preferred to eat beef, pork or lamb, however. Their chat was mostly inconsequential. They were just making noises, really, getting used to each other's sound, to each other's expressions. They both felt so easy in that conversation, as if they had done it all many times before. Their age difference seemed quite unimportant. Later, when Pat suggested that they meet again, maybe for dinner, Elisabeth accepted readily. It was all so natural. They met many times after that. Their friendship blossomed and they began to talk about their interests now that they had established their credentials and got all that out of the way. And so it transpired that both liked birds – rather more, perhaps, than the average lover. Elisabeth had discovered that her spirits rose whenever she drew birds. She almost felt that she should be paying her clients rather than the other way round. Although she had been asked to draw and paint some fabulously colourful birds – and she had enjoyed those tasks enormously – her heart filled when she was tasked with presenting the common Australian magpie.

'A much gentler soul than the thieving magpie of Britain and Europe in general, don't you think?' she askedPatrick with some fervour. He agreed completely. Magpies are probably Australians' favourite bird, so much so that they are readily forgiven for their attacks upon people who wander too near their nests during the few weeks in the year when they are raising their young.

'I love their song too,' Pat replied, 'a sort of bubbly, oggly-oggly-oggly sound. Indeed, I sometimes call them ogglies. Dan thinks I'm a bit loopy, I think. You must meet Dan, by the way. Yes, I am very fond of maggies. I often feed them at home.'

'Yes, I know,' said Elisabeth. Surprisingly, perhaps.

'You know, just about all human cultures around the world have been fascinated by birds from ancient times,' Pat continued in his enthusiasm. 'There have been legends about creatures who were half man, half bird – men with bird heads as well as birds with human heads.

The ancient Egyptian god Horus was one whose story has been told endlessly. Of course, those stories quickly became the vehicles for religious and political dominance. But what I find fascinating about the old stories is their origins before power-hungry kings, queens and emperors stole them. Did you know? The Australian aborigines depicted winged bird-men – and bird-women, too, in petroglyphs, rock carvings – all over the continent. In the Blue Mountains, west of Sydney, in Tasmania – just to name a couple of places. These carvings are some fifteen thousand years old. The aborigines talk endlessly about their "Dreamtime" in which marvellous stories are told about almost anything that they have known or dreamed about. Some measure of authority appears to be anchored in those dreaming stories which have been handed down from generation to generation. Apart from various rock carvings – the bird-men being only some, of course – communication between generations has been oral so that the dreamtime stories have assumed great importance for these people; and, I suspect, for many other societies before the development of writing in one form or another.'

Elisabeth took over: 'The ancient Egyptians had a god of writing, magic, science and knowledge in general, called Thoth who had the head of an ibis. And the soul, which they called the *ba*, was depicted having a human head on the body of a bird. You see, Patrick, I've been studying some of these bird-men as well!' Elisabeth continued now with increasing excitement and charm. 'You know, it's possible that the oldest records of bird-men have been found in the Lascaux caves in France, in the Dordogne. The famous cave paintings there depict not only well-known animals like bison, bears or reindeer, but several bird-men as well. But more, the images show that mental constructs had been created, probably over a long time, before being represented on the cave walls and ceilings, for there is a great deal of evidence to link these images with star constellations; and those certainly took many years of observation to create their associated mental pictures of animals, birds and fishes. The point I'm making is that those cave paintings weren't just happy daubs created at a moment's whim, but had educational and propaganda value rather like the much later use the Egyptians put bird-men to for reasons of religious and political power.'

'In other words, the bird-man idea is almost certainly much older yet,' interrupted Patrick.

'Exactly,' Elisabeth agreed. 'But not only does the notion seem to be incredibly ancient, it is equally pervasive. For example, Hindu mythology talks about the Garuda, the so-called eagle-man who performs as the mount of their god Vishnu.'

'I flew Garuda Airways once,' Pat observed. 'Good to see the name continues.'

Elisabeth was not to be deflected. 'There's a divine being in Japanese mythology called Karura who had a human body and birdlike head. Actually, the name is a transliteration of Garuda and the idea seems to have spread to Japanese culture through Buddhism.'

Patrick was astounded by the breadth of Elisabeth's knowledge and interest in the bird-man story. Until now, he had thought that he alone had a fixation on the subject. Indeed, I have heard his excitement when talking about this subject for years. For Patrick, it was quite wonderful to find someone to share his passion. He was beginning to look on her with newer, dare one say it, more passionate eyes.

Elisabeth was still at full throttle. 'On Easter Island, whose traditional name is Rapa Nui, there was an annual competition to collect the first egg of the season from nests of the sooty tern on a nearby islet called Moto Nui, swim back to Rapa Nui and climb the cliff of Rano Kau to a clifftop village called Orongo. Tangata Manu, from tangata – human – and manu – bird, by the way, was a bird-man who was the traditional winner of that race.'

'That's getting a bit involved, I must say,' Pat replied. 'Maybe he was a bird-fish-man! Anyway, I'm beginning to see where the Iron Man competition began! It's wonderful how many of these stories you know. I have long been aware of some of the ancient Egyptian and Greek stories and I know something of some Russian ones as well, but I had no idea just how widespread the bird-man myth was – and is.'

Confessions

'How did you become interested in the subject, Patrick?' Elisabeth asked. Her tone was rather more intense than simply curious. They had taken up seats next to each other on the sofa in Patrick's home. She looked at Patrick with an affection which seemed disproportionate to the subject of their conversation.

'Ah, well!' Pat replied. 'That's a long story. I guess it began when I was a kid, and as I've come to realise, it has two origins, really. For a start, I have always felt a great affinity with other creatures. Not all, of course; I feel nothing for the insect world – or, if I do, it's more as an afterthought, almost with guilt, you might say – and I suppose I could recite a list of individual creatures with which I feel no interaction. But broadly speaking, I do feel a strong bond with any creature which seems to share my emotional framework. I have, of course, been accused of anthropomorphism but I don't accept the charge. Just look at the unexpected friendships which arise from time to time between individuals of different species, friendships which manifest themselves through gestures and acts which are so like those we make between ourselves. They can be utterly and immediately comprehensible. If a cat can be affectionate to a dog, or a bird to a cat, or a cheetah cub to a domestic dog, why should we feel embarrassment for our affection, or just understanding, of other beings? I would think I'm preaching to the converted on this but when I go on to make supporting noises for pantheism I usually lose my listener's support. I'm aware that there are many definitions of pantheism, which, I must say seem to contradict the very word itself, but all I mean by it is the notion that all things, all creatures certainly, are parts of the whole. If God has any meaning for me, it is merely the idea of belonging to an enormous family, of being a relative, as it were, of every other being – and possibly thing, although I have some difficulties with that.'

'You are getting a bit philosophical, Patrick,' interrupted Elisabeth softly. 'Surely things don't need to be so complicated?'

'No they don't and I don't see things that way. My words might be complicated – I'm probably not expressing things well – but the idea of being part of the whole is surely simple enough. I do hesitate to bring it up really because it's bound to arouse dismissive remarks but it goes some way to express how I *feel* every bit as much as how I *think* about these things. Anyway, I said that my interest in bird-men derived from two sources and that's one of them. The other is that, like so many people, I have discovered, I often have dreams about flying. I've tried to compare notes with friends and acquaintances about the details of these dreams and it is clear that our dreams have much in common. The feeling of soaring above the land, above the trees, into the clouds – the feeling of swooping and diving, and the excitement of taking the short-cuts between places that only belong in the third dimension, as it were – these attributes are, I think, pretty common to dreams of flying. Their origin probably lies in a psychological yearning for flight – a jealousy of the birds' freedom. I don't know about that, though. It's certainly a reasonable idea, a sensible rationalisation of recognised feelings; but that doesn't necessarily make it correct. Anyway, I'm interrupting myself again for I wanted to describe what I also experience in my flying dreams which I have not yet heard from others. Of course, that could just be because I haven't so far met others who share my experience; that is always possible. No; my little twist on this is that I yearn to *teach* others to fly. I can feel muscular urges in my body as I begin to take flight, a sense of stretching my arms, but more particularly my chest, as I thrust off with bended knees; or do I mean, with straightening legs? Then of how it feels to maintain flight, at first with some little difficulty and exertion but then, as confidence grows, with ever greater ease. It's that feeling of *blending* with the air itself so that all heights become equally attainable. Literally, of course, though not without limit. Nothing is without limit. Anyway, I so much want to share my experiences with other people, friends, acquaintances, whoever, to fly like me. All that is necessary, it seems to me, is to instil confidence.'

Elisabeth looked at Patrick as he spoke. Her eyes were quite moist.

He continued. '"You can do it"! I cry out repeatedly. Is that what some bird calls are, I wonder? "You can do it, You can do it"! I never succeed in introducing others into flight in my dreams, however, and that truly saddens me. I realise that I have a gift, that one needs that gift, a gift not given to all or maybe given only to few. I so wish to meet just one other, though. That's my dream, Elisabeth,' he rhapsodised taking her hand in his, 'and thinking of all these stories we have both been retelling about ancient beliefs in bird-men and women, I wonder if they all have their origin in just such a dream as mine. Nothing more complicated than that, despite all the accretions of politics, greed and lust that various societies have deposited over the aeons. Maybe it's all ever so simple.'

'Oh, yes! It is, it is,' gushedElisabeth with such certainty that Patrick felt quite shaken. He didn't know exactly what to say. He had told his tale to others during his life, certainly to me – the same tale, more or less. But never had he elicited such a response before. He had never felt so close to anyone before.

He suddenly felt the urge to confess. 'You know, darling, I really do like birds. I feel a real empathy with them, a kinship, even. I know it's trivial but I like to feed them. I put bread, and meat sometimes, out for them every morning and every evening. I talk to them when they come to eat what I've offered. I feel they like me back, more than just "Here's another sucker to feed us".'

'Oh no! They don't feel that,' she replied, again with an urgency which was truly disturbing.

Patrick continued. 'You know, when I'm dreaming of flying, it's almost as if I am remembering actually being a bird, maybe in a former life. I find the idea of reincarnation very appealing. Provided religion is kept out of it, for that, as far as I'm concerned, is just another way in which institutions and the powerful have tried to bind the common folk. Anyway, I won't go on about that any more.'

'You're getting there,' murmured Elisabeth under her breath. Patrick only heard a faint mumble but her hand held his very firmly.

The Cosmic Lottery

It was many weeks later that Patrick hurried to his now daily meeting with Elisabeth, hardly able to speak in his excitement. Yours truly was actually in on this meeting as it happened. I had invited them both to my place for the afternoon. Elisabeth had already been quizzing me about Patrick's past and our long friendship.

'Goodness me! What on earth is the matter, darling?' she asked. 'You're normally so calm and measured. Are you unwell?'

'Let's have a drink first,' he replied. 'This is going to be a long story! Oh, I'm fine, by the way, it's just that I think I've managed to join the dots.'

Even I, who have known Patrick for most of our lives, was surprised by his urgency, for he is by nature a very calm fellow.

'You know I've had a great interest in astronomy and cosmology ever since I was a boy. I'm sure I told you about that?'

'You did,' she replied, wondering what was coming next.

'I've been doing a lot of reading lately about the fine-tuned universe. You know... '

Elisabeth stopped him in his tracks. 'You must treat me very gently now,' she said. 'I'm no scientist. I *am* interested but you must go very slowly and just give me a general idea. Otherwise, you will lose me and I will surely phase out.'

'Yes, yes. I'm not a physicist or professional scientist myself so we're all going to struggle with this. But let me try – to paint an overview at least.

'I think I'll begin with the idea of units. For example, we measure distance in metres, although we used to use feet and inches. However, the choice of units doesn't matter beyond their convenience. We know, for example, how many feet there are in a metre and we can check that just by putting a metre rule next to one marked in the imperial units. Well we also choose units for mass, usually in grammes; for electric charge, in coulombs; time, in seconds; and so on. There's no relationship between metres, grammes, coulombs and seconds though, because length, mass, charge and time are completely different properties. We can say that units are just a matter of definition and that we have complete control over them – free choice.

'Some typical examples of measures of so-called fundamental quantities are the universal gravitational constant, G; the mass of an electron, m_e; the speed of light, c; in quantum mechanics, Planck's constant, h. Each one of these – and many more – are expressed in terms of so many coulombs, or amps per joule, or joules per tesla; and many more exotic combinations like that. Each of these important quantities – which I haven't named because I don't need to over-complicate the idea I'm trying to put across – has been measured experimentally to a very high accuracy, quite often to within one part in a million, often even more accurately than that. It is, however, possible to make combinations of several of these fundamental constants so that their units cancel and we get a pure number. These dimensionless numbers are the fundamental constants which describe all known interactions in the universe. There are twenty-six of them.'

'A messy situation,' I suggested. Pat and I had talked about this many times before.

Patrick continued. 'So the take-home message at this point is that there are twenty-six fundamental numbers, whose values are known from experiments to high accuracy, which, taken together with the various theories of matter which have been developed over the years, will automatically generate a complete description of everything in the known universe. Scientists are forever on the lookout for ways of reducing this number, as Dan suggests, because they are independent of one another. There are no theories at the moment which relate these numbers to each other. That's rather like saying that there are no known theories at present which can relate certain fundamental theories to others; gravity to quantum mechanics is a popular example, albeit crudely expressed. How are you doing so far, Elisabeth?'

'I'm struggling, Patrick, but I think I'm reasonably OK so far. Are you going to get more complicated, though?'

'Well, how's your quantum chromodynamics? Not good? Nor mine, you'll be relieved to hear, so now we must rely on a few utterly unjustified assertions. Mind you, I've employed several of those already.'

'I'll say!' I interrupted.

'Never mind,' Pat replied. 'I'm only trying to make a sketch. If you want any more, you'll have to sing it yourself, as a song which my father sang many years ago used to go.'

'Take a breath, Patrick,' I interrupted. 'You and I have discussed this so many times that I could say your words for you, so if you'll allow, I'll take over for a few moments. What Pat is getting round to, Elisabeth, is a theory – or it might be better described as a philosophy – that the universe is apparently finely tuned so as to favour life.'

'Come on, Dan, it's not universally agreed by those who accept the fine tuning that there's an anthropomorphic aim to it all,' Patrick interjected.

'I know, I know, Pat, but bear with me for a while. I'll come to that. The central issue, Elisabeth, is that if the various fundamental constants of the universe – those twenty-six numbers – had values only *slightly* different from those we measure – just about everything in the universe would be utterly different. Paul Davies, for example, has argued that if the strong nuclear force were just two per cent stronger than it is, while other numbers remain unchanged, diprotons would be stable so that hydrogen would fuse into them instead of deuterium and helium. As a result, the physics of stars would change utterly and the universe's hydrogen stock would have been consumed within minutes of the big bang. In short, there would be no chemistry as we know it, no biochemistry, no biology, no us.'

'Which might be a good thing, of course,' chirped Patrick.

I was not to be fobbed off, however. 'Martin Rees, a Nobel-prize-winning cosmologist, has discussed the ratio of the gravitational energy required to pull a large galaxy apart, to the energy equivalent of its mass. That's about one in a hundred thousand, by the way, should you want to get cracking and perform some calculations to check things out, Elisabeth.'

'Left my pencil at home,' she said. Her complexion was getting a little pale, I thought.

'Anyway, the point of Rees's argument turns out to be that if that ratio is too small, no stars can form; if too big, no stars can survive because the universe would be too violent,' I continued.

'A fine example of the Goldilocks rule. You know, not too small, not too big, just right,' said Patrick.

'One more,' I continued. 'A fine physicist and cosmologist called Fred Hoyle, who did a great deal of early pioneering work on how stars make various elements, showed that the energy levels of the carbon twelve nucleus – which in turn depend upon several of the values of our fundamental constants – had to take values pretty damn close to those we observe, for if not, insufficient carbon would have been made by the stars to support life.'

'I'm getting saturated,' complained Elisabeth.

'Fair enough,' replied Patrick. 'Let's summarise all this stuff simply by saying that if the fundamental constants in the universe were even slightly different, we wouldn't exist.'

'Why couldn't you have said that in the first place?' complained Elisabeth.

'Actually, because only by blitzing you with complicated and vague notions can we reduce your spirit sufficiently to accept what we have to assert because we don't fully understand it ourselves!'

'That isn't physics; it's psychology!' Elisabeth protested.

'That's true, but I don't quite know how else to get my point across, at the moment. Will you forgive, darling?'

Elisabeth blew Pat a raspberry. 'Alright, carry on with your arm-waving but I reserve the right to ignore your conclusions when the time comes. And may that be soon,' she added.

'Oh, good! Thanks,' said Patrick, glowing. 'Now I can race along. The idea that the universe is tuned for life, Paul Davies argues, is upside down, as it were. It's rather that life has emerged because nature has the fundamental constants that we have measured. Some, you see, had argued that the fine tuning was an anthropic argument in favour of the existence of God...'

'Oh God, he'd have to come in sooner or later, wouldn't he?' complained Elisabeth.

'Ah! But then there are those who argue that the anthropic argument is just teleology,' Pat replied.

'Remind me; what's teleology?' asked Elisabeth. I couldn't blame her.

'Teleology is the philosophical process of arguing that something exists in order that something else may profit. Trees have branches in order that birds may have somewhere to perch, for example,' explained Pat.

'Not a bad idea,' replied Elisabeth, rather naughtily, I thought, but I enjoyed it anyway.

I decided that now was a good point to interrupt Patrick's flow altogether. 'Pat, I have heard you talk about the fine tuning of the universe many times. It's interesting, I agree, but I don't believe that this is the subject that made you come into this room as if your pants were on fire. This is all old stuff to you.'

'Quite right, Dan. It's just that Elisabeth hadn't heard about the idea before and there's a stage I need to get to before I get to the main course. The point, Elisabeth, is that I am not the only one to take a gamble in life. I do the lottery regularly – and the lottery does me, I'm afraid. You should hear Daniel on the subject of the lottery, by the way. No, not now, Dan! No, the point is that nature seems to play the dice too. All that fine-tuning business just shows you how incredibly unlikely it is that the world we know and love should exist at all. You might have thought – quite reasonably, really – that slight changes in those twenty-six numbers wouldn't make much difference to things. Some things would be bigger; somethings would be hotter; some things would be brighter. But, overall, it would have been reasonable to believe that a world much like ours would have come into being even if those twenty-six numbers were a little different. However, it seems that such reasonable intuition is mistaken. It is by one hell of a coincidence that the world, and we with it, should have made an appearance at all.'

'It makes the fourteen-million-to-one lottery odds seem like a certainty,' I interjected. Pat and I had discussed all this many times.

'Exactly,' agreed Patrick, 'so with such incredibly unlikely events like our existence in mind, I can begin to tell you about my latest discoveries.'

'If it's alright with you two, I'd like to suggest we ease the way with another wee drink.' I said, feeling that I was making a worthwhile contribution to this obviously titanic event. Agreement came instantly.

Unlikely Junk

'Elisabeth knows all about my dreams of flying, Dan.' They looked at each other with such an understanding expression that I felt as if I were an interloper. 'She seems to understand and empathise rather,' Pat began. 'Well, I have a confession to make, you two. I have always felt that those dreams were so real and I have so wanted them to be more than just dreams. I have always hoped that they may, to some degree anyway, be *memories*. That I was actually once a bird in a former life!'

'Now you really are getting a bit too fanciful for me, Patrick,' I said. 'I mean, for goodness' sake, let's keep this thing real.' Elisabeth said nothing. I glanced at her for a moment. Her eyes glowed. There was a slight smile on the corner of her mouth.

'Yes, I know, Dan. It's all too much for rational beings like us but try this for size. I've been doing a lot of reading about DNA of late. I was just a young man when Watson and Crick won the Nobel prize in medicine for describing the structure of nucleic acids, and in essence, the key to the hereditary mechanism. That was way back in nineteen sixty-two. That wonderful structure they built showing how it all worked, how certain pairs of bases shared similar lengths that they could form the rungs in a molecular ladder and how the ordering of those base pairs could form a code for the manufacture of proteins in cells. The delightful thing about their work is how the essence of it is immediately accessible to the layman. Of course it's all much more complex than the pop version but anyone, really, can get a rough idea of what it's all about. Their work was followed by a veritable torrent of research papers on the so-called genetic code and on how its information is actually communicated in detail. One of the earliest observations in this field of study was that much, indeed most, it was thought at the time, of the information in DNA strands wasn't important. It was referred to as non-coding DNA. Or as the popular phrase had it; junk DNA. At first, there were objections to the notion that something so wonderful as DNA should be spoiled by long strands of irrelevant stuff, but then it was opined that since the whole thing had presumably come about by random chemical processes by natural selection, there was no reason to suppose that rubbish should not be accidentally included. Indeed, some argued that a totally functional DNA would imply the hand of God; and that did not sit well in the minds of many.

'As time went by, however, it was discovered that much of the "junk" DNA was no such thing, but had different functions than merely coding for proteins. Amongst these are several control segments which can switch the "reproductive" parts on or off; others are regulatory in a variety of other ways, others again appear to have a protective function which can wear out in time and so signal the time of ultimate death. The number of man-years of research which has gone into this area of study is just amazing. You'll be relieved to hear that I have no intention of even trying to sketch that labour. No, the reason why I have even gone as far as this is to tell you about a new line of work which I have been following for some months; and, as you will see, it is the reason for all my excitement.'

'So good to get to the point!' said Elisabeth with a barely perceptible sigh.

Patrick couldn't be stopped now. 'Some scientists in Israel have been studying one particular segment in some human DNA while other workers, this time in Canada, have been doing similar things with avian DNA. The amount of junk DNA varies enormously from species to species, by the way, and it seems that different scientists prefer to work with different species. Their reasons are usually extremely technical but sometimes merely comical. Anyway, it turned out that these two research groups ended up working on *identical* strands of DNA!' Pat waited for this fact to sink in. It seemed not to, however.

'What this means is that there was some human DNA in the bird DNA and *vice versa*! Of course, this may not be a general phenomenon. It may just be a special case for this particular human and this particular bird; or it may be true for a group of humans and a group of birds. A lot more work needs to be done before that is established.'

Elisabeth's eyes opened wide. The penny had dropped! 'What species of bird were they working with?' she asked.

'Australian magpie,' Patrick replied.

She could barely speak. It was certainly the sort of reaction Patrick had sought but her shock and the sudden intensity of her breathing surprised him.

'You see why I'm so excited, don't you?' Patrick said. She barely nodded her head in reply. Tears sprang into his eyes as he continued. 'I really think this all comes together. I have always wondered about the origin of all those ancient bird-man stories. I mean the true origins, not the elaborate veneers of religion or politics. Why did some people even come to imagine that they could fly? Why do I feel that my flying dreams seem more like memories than just inventions or hopes? Could it be that reincarnation is actually more than a religious aspiration? Was I *really* a bird in a former life? And, if so, does that mean that, in some way denied by conventional theories of reproduction, for example, some degree of memory from one life can be carried into another? If reincarnation can occur once, can it occur several times? Or forever?' Patrick was breathing hard by this time. Elisabeth seemed to be similarly consumed by his ideas. 'It's so unlikely, isn't it? But so is the very existence of the whole universe, the stars, our world, us. Much more unlikely than winning the lottery!'

I had listened to all this and watched Patrick's excitement and – what seemed to him – Elisabeth's wonderment. I was inclined to rubbish Patrick on the spot, and indeed had opened my mouth to do so but Elisabeth found her voice.

'Darling, I have been convinced of these things for ages and meeting you after that lecture finally convinced me, because, you see, I have been sure that we have met before. I am certain that we have not done so in the normal way but the feeling that we have met was intense from the beginning. I knew you to be a kind man even before you opened your mouth, and way before your confessions of your affection for birds, which only served to convince me further. You see, you are not the only one with a past, I mean a past life. I too, have been convinced for a good part of my life that I had been a bird, a magpie no less, and what's more, that feeling is so strong that I feel that my being that magpie happened immediately prior to my current existence.' Patrick made to speak. 'No, don't stop me, Patrick. From the moment I met you, I felt that I already knew you. I knew that you bonded with birds – that you liked to feed them. It has been as if you have fed *me*! And, before you bother to make calculations, Dan, I am only twenty-six years old and Patrick is about fifty so it's quite possible from that point of view. Our age difference has never bothered me, simply because I have known him before.'

I couldn't help but ask Patrick, 'Are you saying, my friend, that those bird-men creatures in ancient history – you know, the ones with bodies of humans but heads of birds and so on – are you saying that they really existed?'

'Don't be silly, Dan,' my friend replied. 'Of course they didn't exist. They were just silly inventions of the powerful leaders, and mystics maybe, of those eras. They were simply derivatives of the original dreams and memories that just a few people, I suppose, had described. No, Dan, this isn't science fiction, War-of-the-Worlds stuff I'm talking about. This is *real*. The science behind it is irrefutable.'

I still had difficulty coming to terms with Patrick's tale. 'It just doesn't seem likely though, does it?' I said.

'I guess not... ' he replied, '... statistically. Even less likely than winning that lottery!'